HATTIE MARSHALL
and the
Mysterious Strangers

Other
Hattie Marshall Frontier Adventures
by Debra Smith

#1: *Hattie Marshall and the Prowling Panther*
#2: *Hattie Marshall and the Dangerous Fire*

BOOK 3

HATTIE MARSHALL
and the
Mysterious Strangers

Debra Smith

CROSSWAY BOOKS • WHEATON, ILLINOIS
A DIVISION OF GOOD NEWS PUBLISHERS

Hattie Marshall and the Mysterious Strangers

Copyright © 1996 by Debra Smith

Published by Crossway Books
         a division of Good News Publishers
         1300 Crescent Street
         Wheaton, Illinois 60187

Cover illustration: Doug Knutson

Cover design: Cindy Kiple

First printing, 1996

Printed in the United States of America

Library of Congress Cataloging-in-Publication Data
Smith, Debra, 1955-
    Hattie Marshall and the mysterious strangers / Debra Smith.
        p.   cm. — (Hattie Marshall frontier adventure ; bk. 3)
    Summary: Hattie learns that God's love can heal all wounds when she travels with her mother and grandmother from Texas to Louisiana where they meet a mysterious family.
    ISBN 0-89107-878-9 (pbk. : alk. paper)
    [1. Frontier and pioneer life—Fiction.   2. Caddo Indians—Fiction
3. Christian life—Fiction. 4. Louisiana—Fiction.
5. Indians of North America—Fiction.]
I. Title. II. Series: Smith, Debra, 1955- Hattie Marshall frontier
adventures ; bk. 3.
PZ7.S644685Hap 1996
[Fic]—dc20   95-45121

04	03	02	01	00	99	98	97	96
15	14	13	12	11	10	9	8	7	6	5	4	3	2	1

For Stacey

CONTENTS

1	Fireworks	9
2	A Call for Help	21
3	Errand of Mercy	29
4	Chicken Pox	41
5	Runaway	53
6	Spilled Milk	61
7	Dirty Diapers and Dismal Dreams	69
8	Peace Offering	77
9	Regina	85
10	Birthday Blues	93
11	The Visit	103
12	Medicine Woman	111
13	The Secret	121
14	Confessions	133
	Author's Note	143

1

Fireworks

Hattie could smell the smoke, now wrapping around her as if getting ready to smother her. The heat grew more intense, and her eyes stung and watered as she watched her friend Eric chop at a blazing pine tree. It seemed as if he would never finish so he could join her in the firebreak area.

Somewhere in the forest a tree exploded from the heat that had built up inside it. It sounded like a stick of dynamite, and Hattie instinctively covered her ears. She wanted to run to the McKinneys' cabin and hide. But she stood where she was, paralyzed with fear as she watched the men clear away brush and cut down the burning trees, making them fall away from the cabins and sawmill.

Her brother-in-law Lester Forbes and Mr. McKinney feverishly sawed at a huge chestnut that stood near the firebreak. The top had caught fire and showered them with sparks as Hattie watched anxiously. *Lester shouldn't even be here. If it weren't for*

Rosalie and his mother fussing at each other, he wouldn't be working at the sawmill to earn lumber to build a house for him and Rosalie.

Then through the flames and smoke, she saw another tree fall, like a towering torch—and it was falling straight for Lester!

Hattie tried to scream and warn him, but no sound came from her dry throat. She tried to run, waving her arms, but her body felt like iron and barely moved. Then the tree fell, pinning Lester beneath its flames. She cried out again . . .

"Hattie!"

She bolted upright, wildly trying to grab onto something, anything!

"Hattie Belle, what's wrong?"

It was Gramma. What on earth . . .

Hattie looked around. The flames had been replaced by gray cypress boards and a blue gingham curtain. Instead of blinding smoke, there was a whiff of honeysuckle on the fresh morning breeze. She sighed with relief and sank against the pillow.

"What were you dreaming, honey?" asked Gramma.

"About the fire—again," said Hattie. She was still trembling, and her nightdress was damp with sweat. "It was even worse this time, 'cause when the tree fell on Lester, I couldn't get to him."

Gramma patted her shoulder. "Well, you can stop fretting about that. Lester's burns are healing fine, now that Rosalie's home to take care of him."

"Do you think she'll stay put now?" asked Hattie.

"Sometimes it takes a scare to make folks appreciate what they've got," said Gramma. "I reckon that Rosalie and Lester's mother will try to get along better."

Hattie nodded and stretched, shaking off the nightmare. She had more pleasant things to think about today.

"When will we leave for the picnic?" she asked, hoping thoughts of the day's special festivities would crowd out any memories of the awful dream.

"As soon as the food's ready. Maybe sooner if we have some help," she added, looking her right in the eyes.

Hattie understood and swung her long, slim legs over the edge of the feather bed. Cooking wasn't on her list of favorite chores, but today she'd do whatever it took to get to the picnic. The Fourth of July only came once a year, and she didn't want to miss a thing.

The morning rushed by as food was prepared and carried to the wagon in large oak baskets. Hattie and Gramma held them in place when Papa turned the team onto the steep logging road that led to town. Topping the first hill, they could see the jagged line of evergreens where the fire had stopped north of the farm. Beyond it, a blanket of burned brush and stumps spread across the piney woods, ugly reminders of that frightening day.

It could have been much worse. Thanks to the rain and the fire brigade, no lives were lost. Folks said that Hattie, Eric, and Miriam were bona fide heroes for warning the town and saving Lester. Hattie hadn't felt heroic—just scared. It was good having life return to normal—except for the dreams, of course.

As they approached town, a breeze brought tempting barbecue smells their way. Hattie's skin prickled with excitement as they rounded the last hill. Red, white, and blue streamers hung from a banner stretching across the road, while wagons, buggies, and people on foot moved in irregular waves toward the field behind the church.

When Mama insisted on stopping at Rosalie's, Hattie could bear waiting no longer and left the others behind and ran on ahead. As the crowd thickened, she craned her neck, looking for Miriam and Eric. Finally she spied Miriam's dark, bouncing pigtails.

"Miriam!" she called.

The girl's solemn brown eyes brightened when she spotted Hattie. "I've been looking for you," she announced.

"Mama packed enough food to feed the whole town," said Hattie. "Have I missed anything?"

"Only some races. The band is warming up now."

"Have you seen Eric?"

Miriam shook her head. "I heard that Dr. Siegen was called to the Shelleys' farm this morning.

Someone fell from the hayloft. Maybe Eric went with him."

"Probably," said Hattie. "The doc wants him to learn all he can before going to medical school, even though it'll be a while before he goes."

"I hope they won't miss all the fun," Miriam commented, watching the band.

After a few feeble notes, the music grew louder and more confident while the crowd milled about. A stout figure in a blue and white pinstripe suit, Mayor Stokes, climbed on a small, gaily decorated platform. An American flag flew on one corner, the flag of Texas on the other. The mayor raised his hands as if wanting everyone's attention, but few people noticed as they visited and set out dishes of food. Hattie watched in amusement as Mayor Stokes pointed to someone who *was* paying attention at the edge of the crowd. The second fellow waved back.

"Hattie, where's your bonnet?"

The question came from Mama, who had just walked up behind Hattie and Miriam.

"I forgot it," said Hattie. She hated wearing a bonnet and often forgot to wear it—on purpose.

Mama straightened the thick, coffee-brown braid that hung down Hattie's back, then reached up to feel the top of her head. It was funny, but Mama seemed to be getting smaller every day. Or was Hattie growing taller?

"Well, you're going to get freckles and heatstroke in this hot sun."

"Mama, you know I don't freckle."

"I know. You get brown as a gingersnap, just like your papa." Mama shook her head and handed Hattie a quilt. "Anyhow, go spread this in a shady spot."

The girls wove through the crowd toward a grove of trees.

Ka-boom!

Both girls jumped in fright. Miriam covered her ears. "What on earth was that?"

"The cannon," said Hattie. She looked around. An innocent puff of smoke drifted from the edge of the field. "It usually sits in the town square. This is the only time they fire it."

The band's brassy notes grew stronger, and Hattie recognized "The Star Spangled Banner." She watched the mayor's friend reload the cannon and held her breath as the fuse was lit.

Ka-boom! Flame burst from the cannon's mouth, and another explosion shook the ground.

Hattie grinned at Miriam who finally unstopped her ears, and together they sang the last line: "O'er the la-and of the free and the ho-ome of the braa-ave."

Everyone cheered, and Mayor Stokes raised his hands. This time he had their attention.

"It's an honor to stand before you as mayor of this fine community in the great state of Texas!"

The crowd shouted its agreement.

"Some of you were among the first who settled these hills."

Hattie thought about Gramma as the mayor continued his speech.

"You carved farms out of the forest, fought varmints, starved, and worked your fingers to the bone. You built homes and places of business. Now look at you . . ." He made a sweeping gesture. "Look at us all. With God's help, we've made this a place where others can come to build new lives."

Hattie thought about Miriam, whose father had left Europe for a place where Jews were accepted and not mistreated. And Eric's folks, who had come from Germany to find a healthier, happier life. And she was glad they had.

The mayor went on to talk about railroads and telephones and things less interesting to Hattie than the smell of barbecued meat. At least one person felt the same way and shouted that he could listen to speeches better on a full stomach. Everyone agreed, so Mayor Stokes invited Brother Wallace to ask the blessing.

Everyone bowed their heads, and the preacher prayed, "Dear Lord, we come to You with grateful hearts. Many here today remember the wars fought on Texas soil and are thankful now to be raising their children in peace and freedom. Others know what it's like to be hungry. Thank You for sending rain to save our crops and put out that terrible fire. Please bless America, and lead her in Your eternal ways. Amen."

"This way," said Hattie, pulling Miriam toward a long picnic table crowded with dishes. "We don't want to be the last in line."

Soon their plates were heaped with barbecued ribs, fried chicken, corn on the cob, potatoes, and chocolate cake. Returning to the shady spot they had chosen, they sat down to enjoy their scrumptious meal.

"Isn't your birthday next week?" Miriam asked between bites.

Hattie nodded. "July 12th."

"Are you excited about turning thirteen?"

She sighed. Everyone had asked her the same question, but she had no answer. "If being thirteen meant I could have my own horse and go places by myself, I'd be thrilled; but it won't. Mama will probably decide it's time to teach me more cooking and sewing. At least I'll have a party. Can you come?"

Miriam nodded. "What about courting?" she asked.

Hattie nearly choked on her chocolate cake. "What about it?"

"It won't be long before a boy asks you to a dance or something."

Hattie shook her head.

"It's true," argued Miriam. "You're very pretty, Hattie Marshall, with those blue eyes and dimples. Even my mother says so. It's only a matter of time."

Hattie grunted her disagreement. "You're starting to sound like Rosalie."

"If someone asked you to a dance, would you go?"

"No," said Hattie.

Miriam thought a minute, and her eyes twinkled. "What if Eric asked?"

"That's different," Hattie argued. "He's a friend."

"Ah . . . so you'd go with Eric."

"I didn't say that."

"Well, would you?"

"You're spoiling my dinner," Hattie grumbled, jumping to her feet. "I'm going to get some ice cream."

As the day wore on, people finished eating, and the games began. The greased pig contest was first. Hattie had tried this before and decided to let it pass since she'd forgotten to bring extra clothes. Instead she laughed until her sides hurt as several young fellows chased the slippery hog.

Next came the sack race. Hattie tugged Miriam's arm in encouragement. "Come on. We can do this. It's fun."

"I don't know . . ."

Hattie picked up one of the large burlap sacks. "Okay, put your left leg in . . . Now I'll put in my right one . . ."

"Wait," protested Miriam. "My skirt's coming up."

Hattie hiked the hem of her own blue skirt up around her knees. "Can't be helped," she said. "It's not enough to matter."

"All right, on your mark . . ." called Mayor Stokes.

Nearly twenty sack teams tried to line up straight.

". . . get set . . ."

The girls gripped the burlap with both hands.

". . . go!"

Hattie and Miriam both lunged forward with their right leg—and went down on their knees—hard.

"We have to move *together*," said Hattie, "like this. Sack . . ." Her long right leg and Miriam's shorter left one went forward. ". . . Step . . . sack . . . step."

"We're doing it!" Miriam squealed.

Hattie glanced at the other teams. Some were flat on their faces, while others were making slow progress. Two were far ahead. The crowd was laughing and yelling. The girls pushed on.

One of the leading teams looked back—and tripped. Another pair charged past the girls. They hobbled faster to try to catch up.

"Sack . . . step . . . sack . . . step . . ."

It was hard to say what happened next, but whether it was a hole in the ground or a wrong step, they tripped, going down hard. Miriam hit the ground first with Hattie across her back, her chin bouncing off the back of Miriam's head.

"Oh! What happened?" cried Miriam. "Get off me."

Hattie tried to get up, but her leg was still in the sack. She rolled over and pulled it free, holding her mouth, which throbbed painfully and felt and tasted like it was bleeding. She hardly noticed as the crowd grew louder and the first sack team plunged across the finish line. Mama was beside them in a blink.

"Girls, are you hurt? Hattie, you're bleeding." She whipped out a handkerchief. "Let me see."

Feeling meek, Hattie sat still while being examined. Miriam rubbed the back of her head, which also hurt.

"You bit the inside of your lip," fussed Mama. Her fair cheeks flushed angrily to match her peach-colored hair. "When are you going to stop this tomboy foolishness, Hattie Belle Marshall? You could've knocked a tooth out!"

Hattie could feel her own face growing hot as people gathered around to see the injured girl. Holding the handkerchief to her lip, she climbed to her feet. Miriam was trying to clean the front of her dress. Her mother joined them.

"You girls can clean up at our house," said Mrs. Friedman.

"Good idea," added Mama. "A cold cloth might keep that lip from swelling."

Hattie didn't say anything. It hurt too much. She just nodded, then turned to follow Miriam—and bumped into Eric instead.

"What'r you doin' hur?" she mumbled behind the handkerchief.

"It's a picnic. I thought everyone was invited." He tried to see around the handkerchief. "What's happened to you now?"

She grunted and walked on. Eric followed.

"Do you want Father to have a look? He probably isn't eating yet."

Hattie shook her head, weaving through the crowd behind Miriam and wishing she could disappear.

2

❖

A Call for Help

The afternoon dragged on as the girls watched the picnic from the Friedmans' front porch.

"Don't you want to go back?" asked Miriam. "Even if you can't be in the watermelon-eating contest, we can watch. Maybe you could eat some in little bites."

Hattie shook her head.

Miriam studied the sore lip as if it were a curiosity. "It's puffy," she said, "but not so much that anyone would notice."

"Humph," said Hattie.

"I'm serious. Come look in the mirror."

Miriam got up and tugged at her arm. Hattie knew her friend wanted to rejoin the picnic, so she let herself be pulled into the house. A tall mahogany dresser stood just inside. Hattie stared at the face in the mirror. Her bottom lip was twice its normal size and looked out of place between her thin, straight nose and smooth, tanned cheeks. Her blue-gray eyes were red and the dark lashes wet, as if she'd been crying. It was hard not to, with her mouth hurting and Mama fussing at her in front of the world. And why did Eric have to show up just then?

"It's not so bad," Miriam said gently. "And we almost won."

Hattie nodded. "It was f-fun, 'ut no use going 'ack. Can't eat, can't talk, look stu'id," Hattie said thickly. She tried to pin dark wisps of hair back into her braid and straighten the long bangs. "You go. I'll stay wit' Rosalie."

Miriam hesitated, wanting to go back to the picnic, but not wishing to leave her friend alone. Seeing her friend's dilemma and wanting to make it easier for her, Hattie tromped back outside and down the steps, headed for Rosalie's home.

"Hattie, wait! I don't care about the picnic. We can play checkers or something here."

Hattie just waved and walked on. Rosalie would probably wear her ears out with a big-sister lecture, but Lester would be sympathetic.

"Hattie Marshall!" called a raspy voice.

She turned to see who it was. It was Mr. Beasley, the postmaster, waving an envelope.

"I stopped by the office—a telegram just came in for your folks. Glad you came by. I wasn't looking forward to finding them in that crowd."

Hattie stared at the telegram as if it were a snake. She'd never heard of one bringing good news. "Sam?" she tried to ask.

"Now," he chided, "you know I can't divulge the contents of communications coming through this office. I took an oath." Then, seeing her concern, he went on more kindly, "No, it's not from that cowpunching brother of yours. Is he in Montana yet?"

Relieved, Hattie shook her head and took the envelope.

"Not to worry then. Just give it to your mother," said Mr. Beasley.

Hattie pondered what she should do. She could take it to Rosalie who would find Mama, or she could go back to the picnic herself. Curiosity knawed at her. Finally, with her handkerchief flapping, she turned and ran down the street to the picnic.

Fortunately, people were too busy enjoying themselves to notice her. Those who weren't part of the watermelon-eating contest were busy watching. She skirted the crowd, searching for Mama's yellow bonnet. There she was!

Grabbing her mother's arm, Hattie thrust the envelope in front of her. Mama looked startled; then her green eyes met Hattie's with the same apprehension Hattie had shown moments before. Mama ripped the envelope open and read the telegram aloud: "Millie and kids down with chicken pox. Stop. Help. Stop. Burl."

Mama frowned, but Hattie sighed with relief. She'd had the chicken pox, and she was sorry that Mama's sister and all those little cousins were itching, but it could be worse. Why had her uncle

23

sent the telegram? She looked at Mama with questioning eyes.

"It sounds like your Uncle Burl has his hands full," she said. "I should go . . ."

It was Hattie's turn to look startled.

"How's your lip, anyhow?" Mama pulled the handkerchief down to look, then shook her head. "If it's not one thing, it's two."

"Go *whur*?" Hattie tried to ask.

"To take care of Millie and the kids. Poor Burl must be having a time tending both the farm and the sick babies. Chicken pox can be serious. Help me find your father. We need to talk."

Soon Mama was deep in conference with Papa and Gramma. Hattie listened in silence as plans were debated. Gramma knew all kinds of remedies and felt she should go. Still, it was a long trip for someone recovering from a broken hip. Also, chicken pox could take weeks to go through a family, and there was no way Papa could leave the farm that long.

Hattie wondered where and how she could help the most. She waved and pointed to herself, wondering how she fit into the plans they were making.

Mama thought a minute. "Gramma and I will have our hands full," she said. "We surely could use your help."

Hattie groaned. She didn't like what she was hearing. The last trip to Louisiana, for the birth of Millie's youngest, had been miserable. While it rained outside, Hattie had washed diapers and slept on the floor in the overcrowded house. Then on the trip home she'd fallen in the swollen river and almost drowned.

"Maybe Hattie should stay home," said Papa. "She can be the lady of the house. There'll only be two of us to cook for."

"Nebber mind," said Hattie, having a sudden change of heart. "I'll go!"

Papa winked at Mama. His trick had worked. "How soon can you be ready, Mama?"

"I'll speak to Rosalie and the doc about things we'll need. We'll leave tomorrow morning."

Hattie sighed. At least she wouldn't miss tonight's fireworks.

They were up before the sun, with Mama and Gramma busily cooking provisions for the three-day journey. Once her small satchel of clothes had been packed, Hattie spent spare moments with her animals. Fritter, the burly black pup, whined anxiously. Sitting on the steps, she scratched his silky head, thankful that her lip was nearly back to normal size and she could talk again.

"No, you don't want to go," Hattie explained. "Remember those bad little boys that chased you and pulled your ears at Rosalie's wedding? They'll be there. I doubt even chicken pox will keep them down for long."

Her unhappy thoughts were interrupted by the quiet thudding of hoofbeats. Who would be visiting this early?

A golden-haired rider on a familiar chestnut mare rounded the trees. It was Eric. She met him at the front gate.

"What are you up to?" Hattie knew he was up to something because the indigo eyes sparkled and a smile tugged at his usually serious face.

"How's your mouth today?" he asked.

"Sore but better," said Hattie.

Eric jumped off and handed her a package. "Father sent the salve your grandmother asked for. And . . ." He hesitated, like he was about to give some earthshaking news. ". . . he said I could go with you."

Hattie stared at him, not comprehending.

"He was concerned about the three of you traveling alone, and he also thought I should learn about treating chicken pox."

"Have you had them?" she asked.

"Of course. When I was little. I don't remember it much though." Eric studied her blank face. "What's wrong?"

"You don't know what you're getting into," she warned.

"I'll take my chances," he said thoughtfully. "Besides, I've never been to Louisiana, and I agree with Father about you needing a man along."

He was too earnest for Hattie to laugh. Instead

she led the way into the house, wondering what Mama would say to a fourteen-year-old "man" going along to protect them.

As it turned out, Papa was delighted, and Mama simply nodded in agreement. She was too busy packing to deal with any new thoughts. Once the shock had passed, Hattie was secretly pleased. Maybe having Eric along would make this trip bearable after all.

Since the doc needed his mare back, they stopped at the Siegens' to leave her home and say goodbye on the way out of town. Eric climbed on the wagon seat beside Mama, and as the mules plodded down the cedar-lined drive, she gave him the reins. This bothered Hattie, who had planned to sit there and talk Mama into letting *her* drive the team. After all, she was nearly thirteen!

"Here we are headed for Louisiana, and it's my birthday next week!" she wailed.

Everyone jumped and turned to stare at her.

"What about my party? I'll have to spend my birthday with a bunch of sick people."

Mama frowned. "I'm sorry, Hattie Belle. It can't be helped."

"We can have a fine party when we get back," assured Gramma.

Hattie slumped against the wooden side. It just wouldn't be the same.

3

Errand of Mercy

The sun rose higher and hotter as they bumped along the deeply rutted dirt road. While the recent rains had been welcome, they had transformed the red clay into a slippery mess. The mules had to strain to keep the wagon going up the steep hills, then struggle to keep it from sliding down.

They passed other teams having the same trouble, some slinging mud that splattered against the wagon's canvas top, which Papa had put up to give them shade. The front and back flaps were tied open so a breeze could find its way through. When that happened, the heat was bearable; when the air was still, the wagon became an oven.

Noon passed with only a brief stop to water the team. Mama was determined to cross the river before dark. Hattie could barely get a sandwich into her mouth as they jostled along. She was beginning to think that walking would be more comfortable and started to say so. Then she noticed Gramma.

Damp wisps of gray hair had escaped from her bun and stuck to the thin cheeks, which were tight with pain. Her pale blue eyes were closed as she tried to rest frail-looking limbs on the pillows they had brought along. Unlike Hattie, Gramma didn't have to make this trip; she had chosen to do so because someone needed her. Hattie decided this wasn't the time to complain.

The company of other travelers thinned to an occasional rider, and the hills leveled out as the Marshall wagon approached the river. It was late afternoon before they reached it. Eric stopped the mules as Mama waved to the ferry on the other side. Hattie helped Gramma, her muscles stiff from the ride, climb down, then hopped out for a better look.

The Sabine looked different than she remembered. Instead of a rusty, flooded torrent, the smooth water slid lazily beneath the sun's silver rays.

"Your mother and grandmother swam this wagon across the river with your mules?" asked Eric.

Hattie nodded. "The ferry was gone. The river wasn't peaceful like this either. The Sabine was flooded with a lot of trees and stumps and branches floating in it."

"How'd you fall in?"

"A big log hit the wagon. I lost my balance and fell, and the log rolled into me. I just hung on till it hit a logjam downriver."

"Then what?" asked Eric.

Hattie was silent a minute, remembering how

cold and scared she'd been. "I climbed up on the bank and waited for Sam. He rode all night and found me the next morning."

Eric shook his head. "How do you feel about crossing the river now?"

She thought a minute. "Probably not as nervous as Mama. She doesn't know how to swim."

When the ferry reached them, Mama didn't have a chance to be nervous. She didn't have to be. The mules, remembering their swim across the Sabine, were plenty nervous for her. When Old Droop's foot touched the ramp to board the ferry, he drew back as if it were a snake. The ferryman grabbed his bridle and tried to lead him, but the mule sat back on his haunches, heehawing across the water.

Watching the sun drop, Mama looked exasperated. Hattie calmly fetched a bucket of corn from the wagon and walked ahead of Droop. She picked up a handful and let the hard, yellow kernels dribble back into the bucket. That was music to the old mule's ears, and they pricked forward.

"Come on, Droop," she coaxed. "I know how you feel, but this trip will be different. Here you go. Some good old corn will make it all better."

The mule sniffed, brayed . . . and stood up.

Hattie gave him a bite, then Penny. "That's it. Good mule."

She stepped back, and the wagon moved. His eyes rolling to show the whites, Old Droop cautiously followed her onto the gently rocking ferry.

31

While Mama paid the ferryman six bits for the ride, Eric set the wagon's brake and watched Hattie.

"You'll have them dancing next," he said.

Hattie laughed and fed the mules corn all the way across.

Next they searched for a good place to make camp. The Louisiana side was flatter and swampier, as if the river had once flowed over it. They rode on until gentle hills began to rise and they found a spot where the wagon wouldn't get stuck. After a quick supper of Mama's canned beef, peaches, and sour-dough bread, they settled down for the night.

While Mama arranged the wagon for the wom-enfolk, Eric spread his bedroll near the fire. It felt strange to Hattie to have him there. Swatting mos-quitoes, she brushed her teeth behind the wagon where he couldn't see her. Then she joined him.

"If the smoke doesn't keep the mosquitoes away," said Hattie, "Mama brought extra netting."

"Okay. Thanks."

For once, Hattie could think of nothing else to say. She watched Eric stir the coals, the fire reflect-ing the golden light from his straight, wispy hair. It threw shadows across the high, smooth cheekbones and strong chin, making the boyish face look older. Some of the girls at school thought he was handsome but a little dull, since he was more interested in his studies than in them.

Hattie smiled to herself. Until they'd discovered a common love of fishing, she also had thought Eric too serious to be any fun. But she'd been wrong. Though looks didn't impress her much, she had learned to appreciate his courage, wit, and good heart. Eric might not laugh much, and there was usually a crease between his eyebrows like he was thinking hard. But Hattie knew from the twinkle in those dark blue eyes when he was laughing inside. And when the sensitive mouth did break into a shy smile, it was worth waiting for.

He glanced up to find her staring. "What's the matter?"

"Huh? Oh, nothing. I was thinking about . . . our fishing trips. Maybe Uncle Burl will know someplace we can go."

"That would be nice," Eric agreed. "What does your uncle do for a living?"

"Some carpentry when he's not farming. The extra money comes in handy with all those mouths to feed."

"How many is that?"

"Six. Why? Are you having second thoughts about this?"

Eric shook his head.

"I'm glad you came," she said quietly.

He looked at her for a long moment and was about to say something when Mama called out, "Time to turn in."

Hattie climbed to her feet. "Good night. And watch out for snakes. They have them here in Louisiana, too, you know."

"Thanks," he said. "I'll sleep better knowing that."

Grinning, she climbed into the wagon.

Thanks to the bright rays of morning, Eric woke up first the next day. Hattie could hear him stirring the fire and feeding the mules. Mama closed the wagon flaps so she could dress, and Gramma sat up slowly.

"How do you feel?" Hattie asked her.

"A mite stiff," said Gramma. "These old bones will be glad to get where they're going."

Breakfast was brief, since Mama was anxious to get to their destination, too. She didn't complain, but Hattie could tell by the way she perched on the driver's seat that Mama was tired of sitting.

"Mama, wouldn't you like to trade places a while?" Hattie asked.

Mama glanced back at Gramma and Hattie nestled among quilts, pillows, and supplies.

"Do you need me up here?" she asked Eric.

"No, ma'am," he said politely. Eric was always polite. Hattie couldn't quite understand that.

"All right then," said Mama, "turn left at the next crossroad."

Mama climbed down gingerly, and Hattie hopped into her place. From the high wooden seat she watched lazy mists rise from low-lying areas where tall cypress trees spread feathery green limbs draped with lacy Spanish moss. A flock of spindle-legged white egrets flapped into the air as the wagon rattled by; the other birds tried to outdo one another in morning song.

Hattie was so entranced that Eric startled her when he spoke. "Father said we'd be traveling *El Camino Real*, the King's Highway. Is this it?"

"I don't know," said Hattie. "Gramma, is that what they call this road?"

"It sure is," Gramma answered. "But this road ran from Natchitoches, Louisiana to Nacogdoches, Texas long before the Spanish named it. It was a trail connecting two groups of the Caddo Indians. The towns are named for them."

"I've wondered about those names," said Eric. "This part we're on now—was it Spanish or French territory?"

"Both." Gramma chuckled. "Texas was once part of Mexico, and France claimed Louisiana. Later, when Louisiana became part of the U.S., they couldn't agree on a boundary. The land between became the Neutral Zone and filled up with bandits. Traveling through, like we're doing now, got so dangerous they called it 'No Man's Land.'"

Hattie's skin prickled as she gazed across the wooded hills. "Are any of them still here?"

"No, Hattie Belle, that was a long time ago," said Gramma assuringly.

Hattie wasn't sure whether she was relieved or disappointed.

Watching Eric jiggle the long reins reminded her

why she'd wanted to sit there in the first place. Leaning his way, she whispered, "Let me drive."

His eyebrows, darker than the wispy gold hair, knit together in a frown. "Why?" he asked.

"To show Mama I can." Her slim, brown fingers slipped across his larger ones to touch the reins. "Please?"

Eric stared at her hand, and something inside Hattie told her that he couldn't refuse. Taking a deep breath, he passed the leather thongs to her.

Hattie smiled and took them confidently. The mules plodded on as Mama and Gramma chatted, then settled down for naps. It would be a while before they noticed the change in drivers, and by then Hattie could prove herself capable of handling the job.

They came to the crossroad and veered left. Turning the team wasn't much harder than reining a horse you sat on. Hattie felt a glow of pride—and annoyance at Eric for sitting so close. Was he waiting to grab the reins or just blocking Mama's view, for Hattie's sake?

This section of road looked lonely and less traveled. Deep ruts had been cut, probably by a logging crew.

Afraid the road was too rough for Hattie, Eric reached for the reins. He got her elbow instead.

Just then a back wheel hit one of the ruts, jerking the wagon hard. Hattie could feel her bottom bounce off the seat and held her breath, waiting for Mama to sit up and say something. But she didn't.

Relieved, Hattie took a deep breath and guided the mules to the left side of the road. No problem. She knew how to avoid the ruts now. Refusing to look at Eric, she could feel the blue eyes boring holes into her head.

"You'd better give me the reins," he whispered. "This part can get a little tricky."

Hattie ignored him and tightened her grip on the leather reins until her knuckles turned white. This might be the most fun she would have on the whole trip.

She studied the road. The left side was smooth enough to go a bit faster. She jiggled the reins. Normally she would have clucked to the team, but then the women in the back would know she was driving. She shook the reins again until they bounced across the mules' chocolate-colored backs.

Droop tossed his head in protest but broke into a trot. Penny did the same. The wagon bounced even harder than before with the increased speed.

Hattie smiled as a warm breeze fanned her. She was elated. This was the next best thing to riding a horse—and far more grown-up.

"Slow down," Eric growled beneath his breath, "or I'm telling your mother." His tone of voice conveyed definite concern, but Hattie wasn't about to give up the reins.

She glared at him, hoping he would leave things be.

The road began going downhill sharply, and the

mules picked up even more speed. Hattie didn't want to bounce Gramma too much, so she pulled back on the reins. But Old Droop was hot and annoyed now and didn't seem to care what Hattie wanted him to do.

Gritting her teeth, Hattie pulled harder. She saw that at the bottom of the hill the road curved sharply to the left. They would have to slow down to make the turn safely.

"Whoa, Droop," she whispered, not wanting Mama to hear. The mule acted as if he didn't hear either, tossing his ornery head and going faster yet. In just a few moments they would be in the curve. Hattie's heart began beating faster.

She kept a silent, steady pull on the reins. Eric reached for them again, but she leaned away from him. She could handle this, she hoped.

Mama stirred in the back. "Aren't we going a bit fast?" she called anxiously. She was only a little worried because she thought Eric was still driving.

When Droop broke into a lope, Hattie considered shoving the reins into Eric's hands, but her pride wouldn't let her. Still, she had to do *something*, even if Mama knew she'd been driving and was the cause of the problem. Pulling the reins back tight, she yelled, "Whoa!" It didn't help.

Now they were approaching the bottom of the hill at breakneck speed. Hattie leaned away from Eric again, but he stood up so he could reach around her, and he snatched the reins away.

It was too late. With the mules in a full hoof-pounding, bone-rattling gallop, they hit the curve. The animals swung left as if they weren't pulling anything. Eric, knowing that a sharp jerk to the left would turn the wagon on its side, yanked with all his might, trying to keep the mules going straight, even if it meant running into the woods. Both he and Hattie couldn't help but think about folks they'd heard about who had been killed when their wagons overturned.

The mules' heads popped back when they felt Eric's muscles tugging on the reins. Hattie would have been annoyed if she weren't so busy praying. *I'm sorry, Lord. Please keep us from turning over!*

The wagon jerked and leaned, groaning in its wooden joints, and for a long, terrible moment they rolled along only on the right wheels. Eric yelled at the mules while behind them Mama screamed and boxes tumbled. Unable to turn around or even breathe, Hattie hung on in fear.

After what seemed like a very long time, the mules listened and swerved to the right. The wagon settled back on all fours with a loud *thud!* They were still moving, however, and Hattie wondered how far the team might carry them into the woods.

When the wooden wheels hit the deep ruts on the right side of the road, the wagon began lurching crazily, and the mules kept pulling.

Eric kept yelling "Whoa!" as Hattie gripped the high wooden seat that threatened to tumble her off.

They all heard a loud *pop* as a wheel snapped under the strain, causing one corner of the wagon to fall heavily. The women inside the wagon cried out amid the sound of breaking glass. Finally, after dragging the crippled wagon a long ways, the mules came to a stop.

4

Chicken Pox

For a long, breathless moment, no one spoke. Then they all started at once.

"What happened?" Mama shrieked.

"Gramma, are you okay?" called Hattie.

"Is anyone hurt?" yelled Eric.

"How's the wagon?" Gramma wanted to know.

As Eric jumped off to grab the mules, Hattie climbed over the wagon seat. Her mouth dropped in dismay. It was as though the two women and all their things had been shaken together in a cracker box. Baskets were upside-down, the food scattered about; the clothes satchels had landed on Mama, who shoved them aside and tried to stand on the tilted floor. Her strawberry-blonde bun hung cock-eyed on her head, and Hattie cringed before her mother's red face and blazing green eyes. Mama was so angry that her voice shook as she spoke.

"What did you think you were doing, Hattie Belle Marshall? You could have gotten us all killed!"

Hattie was trying to think of an answer when she looked at Gramma. The wooden crate of peaches had been thrown against her, covering her side of the wagon with broken glass and syrup.

"Oh, no . . . Gramma, wait! Let us help you," cried Hattie.

"Grab that quilt, and we'll mop up this syrup," said Gramma. "Watch the glass now."

Hattie scrambled to obey. Then she saw a large, purple knot on Gramma's arm. "What happened?"

"That box gave me a lickin'," said Gramma.

Hattie wanted to cry. "I'm so sorry," she whispered. "I'd never hurt you for anything. I—"

"I know that, honey. It's just a bruise—nothing to worry about," Gramma reassured her. "Here—help me up."

Hattie helped her get out of the wagon. They stepped over to Mama, who was surveying the damage with Eric.

"How long was Hattie driving?" Mama was asking him.

"The last three or four miles," Eric confessed. "But, Mrs. Marshall, it's my fault for letting things get out of control."

Hattie drew a deep breath, and they both looked her way. Eric's jaw was clenched tight, and his blue eyes shot darts at her.

"No, Mama, it was my fault. I pestered him into letting me drive."

"It was a stupid, willful stunt," said Mama. "What were you thinking of?"

Hattie felt hot all over, like a leaf wilting beneath an angry summer sun. The trouble was, she hadn't been thinking at all.

"Just to show you I could do it," she muttered. "I'm really, really sorry."

"Well, saying sorry won't change this broken wheel," Mama snapped. "Help Eric take it off while I unbolt the spare one. I just hope the axle is all right."

Hattie could see that the wheel stuck in the rut had snapped into kindling, and the axle was slightly bent. After lots of hammering, they gathered to raise the wagon as Gramma pushed the good wheel into place. As Hattie watched Eric work, she realized he probably could have done it alone. Taller than she was, having a medium build, he was used to hard work. When he wasn't studying, his mother kept him busy with her garden and flower beds. And he was naturally healthy and strong.

Hattie wondered what he was thinking about now. He wouldn't even look her way. Had she ruined their friendship with her selfish stunt?

Mama seemed to be in a better mood once the wagon was upright. Precious time had been lost, so she moved the team out quickly. Hattie quietly curled up in the back with Gramma, the only person not angry with her, and pretended to take a nap.

When they camped at dusk, she felt more comfortable tending the mules, away from everyone else for a while. Mama still wasn't saying much to her. And Eric had said nothing at all. Hattie thought back to the morning after the fire, when they had felt so close and were applauded as heroes. She was amazed that she had gone from friend to foe, from heroic to humiliated, in such a short time.

The next day found them on the last leg of the trip. Mama let Eric drive again as she talked quietly, preparing him for what lay ahead.

"Millie's my youngest sister," Mama was saying. "She was just a baby when our folks left Georgia after the War. I was about five. We sailed around to Galveston and hadn't been there two weeks when yellow fever broke out."

Mama shook her head and was quiet a moment. "It took our parents, our older sister, and two brothers. Some friends, the Barnums, had come on the same boat and took us in and raised us. They built a store in Galveston, so we lived down there until we both married. Millie and Burl love young'uns, and they have a lively bunch, believe me. I don't know how she manages, but when she needs me I always try to go. It's funny how I wound up on one side of the Sabine River and Millie on the other."

Eric was thoughtful. "Father has told me about the yellow fever epidemics down on the coast. I'm glad chicken pox isn't as serious."

44

"So am I," said Mama. "But it's still no picnic. It was good of you to come with us. We'll need the help."

Eric shrugged, and his voice was so low that Hattie could barely hear him. "I wasn't much help yesterday. I hope you'll forgive me for letting Hattie drive. It's just . . . Well, it's hard saying no to her."

Mama's shoulders jerked as if she were laughing. "Yes, I suppose it is."

Hattie's mouth dropped open, not knowing whether to be indignant or pleased. Gramma, whom she thought was asleep, just smiled.

They reached Millie's at noon. After winding along a narrow, bumpy drive, the woods suddenly gave way to a spacious yard and fields in various stages of harvest. A short picket fence surrounded the white, clapboard house with the spacious L-shaped porch. Uncle Burl's skill was evident in the decorative woodwork, which seemed out of place on such a remote homestead.

Hattie knew right away that something was wrong. Instead of the cousins rushing out to greet them like a flock of little chickens, the yard was still. From the house came the thin wail of a baby. Mama pulled up to the gate and rushed inside without pausing to give further orders.

"What should we do?" asked Hattie, dreading to go in.

45

"Unload the wagon and put the team up," Gramma said as Eric helped her down.

Not looking at each other, she and Eric piled the belongings by the gate. Then Hattie led the mules behind the barn where the wagon would remain until it was time to go home. She hoped it wouldn't be long.

Together they unhitched Droop and Penny and found two empty stalls. The barn was large and was cluttered with a conglomeration of tools. Hattie shook her head, wondering if Uncle Burl ever threw anything away. When the mules were settled, she decided to speak to Eric. Even if he didn't talk back, he couldn't help hearing what she had to say.

"Eric, I'm sorry about yesterday. I really appreciate you letting me drive, and I'm sorry I made Mama mad at you."

He didn't even look her way.

Hattie stomped her foot in frustration. "Ignoring me doesn't change anything. I was having fun and got carried away. It won't happen again, okay?"

Eric sighed. "It was a dumb stunt. But I should know by now to expect that from you."

Her face got hot with sudden anger. Maybe not speaking *was* better. Spinning on one heel, Hattie marched to the house.

Her oldest cousin met her at the door. Hattie stopped, staring. "Clovis?"

"Hi, Hattie," he said hoarsely. Nine-year-old

46

Clovis had his father's light brown hair and square, good-natured face. At the moment it was covered with red eruptions.

Hattie had forgotten how awful the chicken pox were. She had only been five when Sam and Rosalie caught them at school, and then Hattie got it from them. Rosalie had been so upset with her looks that Mama hid all the mirrors. Hattie mostly remembered the itching. Now she tried not to cringe as Pearl, who was seven, ran to hug her.

"Uh, hi," said Hattie. Pearl was skinny and red-headed like Aunt Millie, and the bright spots matched her hair.

"Mama says you've already had the chicken pox so you can't get 'em again so you can stay with us," Pearl said in one breath. "I'm so glad you're here, 'cause Mama's in bed and Daddy can't cook a lick."

Hattie tried to smile as she patted the silky red head. Then she looked closer. "They're in your hair?"

"*Everywhere*," said Pearl. "It's awful."

Hattie nodded sympathetically. "Where are the other kids?"

"In bed," said Clovis. "They still have fever. Pearl and me got sick first at school. Then Mama about a week later, and now the little 'uns."

Together they went through the living room to a large bedroom the boys shared. The twins, Ben and Billy, were wrestling on the tall feather bed.

47

"Quit that! You're gonna fall off again," ordered Clovis.

The four-year-olds paused to grin at Hattie, the freckled patches across their stubby noses blending with the pox to form comical patterns.

"Hey, Hattie, did you bring Fritter?" they chimed.

Hattie shook her head, glad for the one good decision she'd made about this trip. "How do you boys feel?"

"Fine," said Billy.

"Terrible," yelled Ben. "My ears itch, my feet itch, my . . ."

"We know." Clovis cut him short and pointed Hattie through the door. Behind them the noise continued.

"I said we felt fine," Billy argued.

"No, we don't. We feel awful!"

Billy grabbed his brother's head, and the bed-springs groaned as they continued their wrestling. Clovis shook his head.

"It sounds like they need to go outside," Hattie commented.

"Daddy says not till the fever's gone or they could get ammonia like Momma," said Pearl.

"Get what?" Hattie was confused. Maybe Pearl meant the ammonia-like fumes coming from a pile of wet diapers in the back room.

"She means *pneu*monia," corrected Clovis.

"Mama came down with it. That's when Daddy sent the telegram."

They entered Aunt Millie's room quietly. The curtains were closed, and it took their eyes a moment to adjust to the dimness. Aunt Millie's fluffy mattress was so piled with quilts that it was hard to find her. But a hard cough and raspy breathing gave her away. As they drew near, her eyes opened. They were green like Mama's, but the sparkle had vanished. Her pale cheeks had turned pasty, and the dark auburn hair spread across the pillow in tangled knots. Hattie had never seen anyone look so ill.

"Hattie Belle," she whispered, reaching out a painfully thin hand. "It's good to see you."

Hattie started to say something polite but choked on the words. She held the white hand gently and cleared her throat.

"You don't have many spots, Aunt Millie," was all she could think to say.

Aunt Millie tried to smile. "Thank you for coming to help with my babies," she said.

Hattie nodded, feeling guilty because she hadn't really wanted to come. "You rest now. I'll see what Mama wants me to do."

Clovis and Pearl followed her in a solemn procession to the kitchen. Gramma already had a pot of herbs boiling for her special tea and was instructing Uncle Burl on how to cook the hen he had plucked for chicken soup. With baby Michael on one hip,

Mama was trying to pour a bottle of milk. Winnie, the two-year-old, sat scratching in the corner and whining pitifully.

"Hattie, there you are!" Mama looked relieved. "Bring in that box of canned goods, and open a jar of peaches. That will hold them until we can tend to Millie and cook dinner."

Uncle Burl ruefully smiled. "It's sure good of you gals to come help us out. I was getting desperate."

Hattie started to say that she could see why, then thought better of it. Going after the box of food, she met Eric at the front door.

"How is everyone?" he asked.

Hattie just shook her head.

Like generals ordering troops around, Gramma and Mama had things in reasonably good shape by suppertime. Hot breathing concoctions turned Aunt Millie's room into a steamy pine forest with the sharp twang of mustard plaster added for good measure. Hard coughs still wracked her body, but the tea and soup had brought some color back to her cheeks.

Once fed, the four younger children were bathed in soda water to relieve their itching, while the worse spots were covered with a healing salve. Hattie couldn't decide who had the most or looked the strangest. When the twins had finally worn themselves out and the women sat down to rock the babies, she escaped to the cool porch. Except for an occasional mosquito, all was quiet.

"It's been a long day," came Eric's voice through the darkness.

She peeked around the corner of the porch. "I thought you had already turned in," said Hattie. "You're lucky, sleeping in the barn. I have a pallet in the living room."

"I'll tell the mules you miss them," he said.

Hattie sighed. She missed a lot more than the mules. As the wooden rockers creaked in harmony with a chorus of crickets and the occasional boom of a bullfrog, she was glad that something here resembled home.

"Uh . . . Hattie?"

"Yeah?"

"What are you doing first thing in the morning?"

"Mama told me to wash all their clothes. The diapers alone should take two days. Why?"

"I may need your help with a chore. It won't take long."

Hattie stopped rocking and glanced curiously around the corner. He sounded positively meek. "Like what?" she asked.

"Well, your uncle is leaving early, driving to town for supplies. He asked if I'd tend the livestock and work the peas. That's fine, except for one thing."

"What's that?"

"I . . . I've never milked a cow. My mother likes chickens, but we've never owned a cow."

51

Hattie grinned to herself. Mr. Know-it-all Siegen needed her help!

"I don't know," she chortled, "I might pull another dumb stunt and you'd get blamed for it."

"Never mind," he said crossly. "I'll figure it out."

She chuckled at the thought. "I wouldn't miss that for the world."

5

Runaway

Hattie didn't know why she had worried about waking up early. Long before daylight the baby's crying and Winnie's plaintive howl roused the whole house. Baby Michael was hungry, but Winnie just itched. The way she couldn't keep troubles to herself, the two-year-old reminded Hattie of Rosalie and her willingness to share misery. As Mama tended the baby and Gramma fixed a soda bath, Winnie sat whining at the foot of Hattie's pallet. No wonder Uncle Burl was cheerful this morning—he was leaving for a few hours.

"Don't fret, Winnie. Gramma's fixing a nice bath to make you feel better."

"No baff!" she wailed. "Spots hurt."

"I know." Hattie patted the fluffy brown head. "But it makes them better. Do you have a toy to play with in the water?"

Winnie shook her head.

"Let's find one then." Hattie stiffly climbed to

her feet. The floor had been hard. She stumbled in the semi-darkness to the kitchen, where she found a small tin cup with a curved handle. "Here we go. We'll pretend this is a boat on the river. Now where's the water?"

Winnie pointed to the bedroom, where Gramma was mixing soda with lukewarm water in a small washtub. Hattie led the way and made the "boat" sail around the tub. Gramma slipped off Winnie's tiny nightdress. Hattie cringed. Ugly red blisters glared from tender white skin across the child's chest and stomach.

"Some of these are infected," said Gramma. "They'll leave scars."

Hattie shook her head and grabbed Winnie's hand as she started to scratch. "Let's play with the boat instead," she said gently. "Come on . . . In you go."

Before the child could argue, Hattie scooped her up and into the water with a small splash.

"Owww-ww!"

"Watch out. You'll sink the boat," warned Gramma. Holding Winnie firmly, she winked at Hattie. "I'll manage now. You can see to the chores."

"Yes, ma'am." Remembering Eric and the cow, she dressed quickly and ran to the barn. The door was open. They were gone.

For a moment Hattie just stood there uncertain of what to do. Where would Eric have taken her? Then as her eyes adjusted to the barn's dim light, she noticed the milking stool upside-down and the bucket lying several feet away. A tangled rope halter hanging from a post told the rest of the story. Eric had no idea what to do with a cow, but the old jersey had apparently known what to do about him.

Untying the halter and lead rope, Hattie darted outside to look around. Human footprints were everywhere, but fortunately only one cow was out. She soon found large cloven hoofprints in the red earth leading down the hill into the forest. They were easy to follow in the wet sand along a creek that wound through the woods. Half a mile from the house the creek dropped sharply into a ravine, and the tracks disappeared. The hill that rose in front of her seemed the reasonable way to go, but she couldn't be sure. The ground was harder here and wore a thick carpet of leaves and pine needles that left no prints.

"Eric!" she called, then listened. The birds grew quiet.

"Er-ri-ic! Where are you?"

There was no answer. Where could they be? Guilt and worry tugged at Hattie. She could have agreed to help Eric without teasing him—and she definitely should have told Mama before taking off through the woods.

"Lord, here I go again," she muttered, trudging up the hill. "Running off on half a brain. Gramma says that you give wisdom to folks just for the asking. Well, I'm asking now. I'd hate to get Eric in trouble, or to have him mad at me again; well, I guess just in trouble—he's already mad. Please show me what to do."

Reaching the top of the hill gave her a better view of the forest. Where would a cow want to go around here? The woods grew thicker, broken by an occasional clearing. She remembered the old saying about birds of a feather flocking together and wondered if Uncle Burl's ornery cow was seeking a friend. He'd never mentioned another farm nearby. When the baby was born last fall, the folks that came to visit were mostly from town.

Hattie sighed and, shielding her eyes from the morning sun, looked toward the east. Fog rose from a low area farther down the creek. Or was it fog? She strained to get a better look, and her eyes watered in the glare. A line of gray smoke drifted upward from a thin area of trees.

She started down the hill toward it. It might be nothing at all, or it could be a farm with cattle. If she were a runaway milk cow, reasoned Hattie, that's exactly where she'd go.

After hiking some distance through a wooded tangle, Hattie found herself on a narrow trail above the creek. The rustle of leaves startled her as an armadillo scurried away. Then a low thudding and a dog's bark stopped her cold.

Hattie gripped the halter and waited. The noise grew louder, making her heart beat faster. Then came a crackling of limbs as a large, bony head burst through the trees, pounding right toward her.

"Whoa!" she cried, waving the halter.

The cow bellowed and turned aside, plunging down through the creek. A small brown and white dog barked and nipped at her heels as she disappeared up the other side.

Eric wasn't far behind. "Come back, you . . ." he yelled.

"You'll never catch her like that." Hattie laughed with relief.

Eric's face was beet-red and his white shirt dark with sweat as he skidded to a halt beside her. "I'd almost caught her when that dog showed up," he panted. Noticing the halter, he relaxed a bit. "Do you have a better idea?"

"Maybe," said Hattie, "but cool off first."

He nodded, and they walked down to the creek where the water ran cool and clear over a sandy bottom. Hattie didn't realize how thirsty she was. They drank deeply and rinsed their arms and faces. Then Eric sat down to catch his breath.

"I almost hate to ask," said Hattie, "but what happened?"

Eric snorted. "Old Bossy didn't like the way I did things."

"Her name isn't Bossy. I think it's April."

"Well, excuse me," said Eric, folding his arms in disgust. "That must've been the problem—we weren't properly introduced."

Hattie grinned. "You should have tied her in the

stall and fed her. Cows generally like to eat while they're being milked."

"I'll try to remember that," he said crossly, then looked at Hattie. "Thanks for coming anyway."

She shrugged. "I should've helped you. I'm sorry I didn't. But we need to get back. I didn't tell Mama where I was going."

Eric grunted and climbed to his feet. "Okay. But which way did *April* go?"

"If you're looking for the cow," came a soft, low voice, "my dog ran her back to our place."

Hattie and Eric both jumped. *Who was that?*

At first they saw no one. Then a shadowy shape emerged from the trees. Faded overalls covered thin, bare shoulders, and the darkest eyes Hattie had ever seen peered at them beneath a thick mop of black hair. The face was round, smooth, and the color of Mama's gingerbread.

Eric found his voice. "Where did you come from?"

The boy, who looked to be about ten years old, pointed up the creek with a short piece of sugarcane. "My place."

Then Hattie remembered the thin line of smoke she'd seen earlier. "You have a farm?"

The boy nodded.

"If you'll show us the way," said Eric, "we'll take the cow home."

The boy turned to lead them up a faint trail. Hattie noticed that his leather shoes, which were hand-sewn, made no sound on the leaves.

"I'm Hattie, and this is Eric," she said, trying to remember her manners. "We're from Texas."

"I'm Peter Varga," said the boy.

They followed him along the twists and turns of the creek, then climbed a gently sloping hill. As they approached the top, the thick trees opened into a clearing. A wooden frame house stood in the middle with chickens scratching about. Hattie stopped to stare. Something was different about the house, but what? Then she realized that unlike her home and Aunt Millie's, this cabin sat right on the ground and had no windowpanes. Thick wooden shutters were propped open to let a breeze pass through.

Peter led them to a shed in the back. Gray Spanish moss had been hung to dry across one side, almost obscuring a man hollowing a thick cypress log with a small ax. Suddenly feeling shy, Hattie wished they could just find April and go home.

"Pa, these two are looking for the cow Deetsi brought in," said Peter.

The man raised up to study them before speaking. He was no taller than Hattie and was squarely built. Wood chips covered his loose-fitting work clothes. The eyes were dark and deep-set, but not unkind.

"Did you lose something?" he asked.

"Yes, sir." Eric stepped forward and confidently offered the man his hand. "I'm Eric Siegen. A milk cow I was tending got away. If she's here, we'll be glad to take her along."

Hattie had to hand it to Eric, who could be terribly mature when he tried. He certainly hid being nervous and embarrassed better than she could.

The man's dark eyes twinkled, and he almost smiled. Shaking Eric's hand, he said, "I'm Lou Varga. Was it you making all that racket in the woods?"

"I had a little help from your dog," said Eric. "But it's okay. I've been chasing that cow since daylight."

"Then you must be hungry. Peter, see what Enah has left from breakfast." He pointed to Hattie. "What about you?"

"I'm Hattie Marshall, and I guess I'm hungry, too. But we don't want to be any trouble, and we need to get home."

"Where's that?" he asked.

"Sabine County, Texas," she answered without thinking.

"You chased a cow all the way from Texas?" asked the man.

"Oh no," Hattie explained. "My aunt and uncle own the farm about a mile south of here. Maybe you know them—the Cottons?"

Lou Varga shook his head no and leaned over his work. "Go along with Peter. He'll fix you up."

6

❖

Spilled Milk

Hattie was hungry, but she also knew Mama was probably worrying about where she was. She threw Eric a worried frown. "We need to go back," she whispered.

"We can't be rude," he whispered. "This won't take long."

They followed Peter into the cabin, where morning sun streamed through in hazy shafts of light. Hattie squinted as her eyes adjusted to the shadows and the thin wisps of smoke. It came from a small cookfire in the middle of the floor. Something was different here. Then she realized what it was—the house had no chimney. Hattie was staring at the roof, pondering this mystery, when Peter cleared his throat.

"Enah," he said, "these two came after the cow. Pa said to feed them."

Only then did Hattie notice a woman seated at a table in the shadows. As she rose, the light glinted across her hair, which was the rich color of pewter and was drawn back in a bun. But what drew Hattie was the deeply lined face that reminded her of soft, tanned leather stretched over high cheekbones. The deep brown eyes studied Eric and Hattie closely. People usually didn't intimidate Hattie, but something in this ancient woman's gaze made her feel as small as Winnie.

The woman, who had to be the grandmother, finally spoke. "Who are you?" she asked.

"She's Hattie, and I'm Eric," he said quickly. "And we don't want to be any trouble."

"Wash there," said the woman, motioning them to a bucket of water and a towel in the corner.

Hattie could feel the dark eyes resting on her as she washed her hands. It was the same when she and Eric sat at the table.

"Regina, get the bowls," she said to the shadows.

Hattie was surprised to see another figure move away from a bench attached to the wall. The girl was sitting cross-legged there with a sewing basket. Quickly she unfolded slim legs and fetched two bowls from a shelf. These she handed to the woman, who dipped something from a pot over the fire.

Then it was Hattie's turn to stare. White china bowls filled with something like grits were set before them next to objects she had never seen on a table before—cow horns. Hattie picked one up, turned it in her hand, and looked at Eric questioningly.

At first he seemed just as puzzled. Then understanding came into his eyes, and he dipped the horn into his bowl. Hattie watched as the wide, hollow end scooped up a mouthful of the food. Holding the horn's narrow, curved end, Eric maneuvered the horn to his mouth and smiled. Hattie carefully did the same and found the hot corn mush to be tasty.

Peter, who had watched them curiously, sat down before a small basket of wild plums and plopped one into his mouth. Regina stood by quietly. Now that she was closer, Hattie realized that though she was small, the girl was probably in her mid-teens. Her thick, black hair was parted in the middle, framing a heart-shaped face; the dark, thick-lashed eyes followed their every movement. Hattie wanted to ask a dozen questions but didn't know where to begin.

The woman beat her to it. Settling her broad body on another chair, she watched them intently. "You like the food?" she asked in her low voice.

Eric nodded. "Thank you. I've been chasing that cow since daylight. That works up an appetite."

"Where did you chase her from?" the woman asked.

"My aunt and uncle's farm," explained Hattie. "About a mile south and across the creek. I'm surprised you don't know each other. My cousins complain about not having many neighbors."

The woman just grunted.

Hattie dipped into her bowl again. "This is a neat spoon."

Peter grinned and offered her a plum. "You look like you've never used one before."

"Well, I haven't," said Hattie. "At least, not like this."

Peter cocked his head. "So what do you eat with?"

A bit confused, Hattie was opening her mouth to tell him when a whirlwind of a person came rushing through the door.

"Inez, be careful with those eggs!" warned Regina.

The small girl clutched her basket as she skidded to a halt. One egg bounced free and landed on the dirt floor with a splat, but she hardly noticed, she was so busy staring at Hattie and Eric with her huge brown eyes.

"Did you bring us the new cow?" she asked them. "I was out looking for the hen's new nest, and when I got back, there the cow was. She's really fat."

Hattie started to explain, but Regina moved between them, muttering like a flustered chicken as she scooped up the broken egg. "When will you learn to *walk* with the eggs? And to not speak before you're spoken to? Now give me that basket and calm down."

Hattie had to smile at quiet Regina's exploding into a "big sister" lecture. It sounded so much like her and Rosalie.

Apparently Inez was used to it, because she just kept rattling on. "So who are you anyway?" she asked

Hattie. "I've never seen you before. Why would you bring us a cow? Did Pa buy it?"

"Be quiet, little one," the woman gently scolded. "The cow ran away, and they will take her home."

"Oh." Inez sagged a bit. "Since our cow had fever, her milk's bad and we can't drink it. I thought maybe . . . Never mind."

"I'm sorry about your cow," said Hattie.

"It's all right," said Peter. "We have a heifer who's having a calf soon. She'll have enough milk to share."

Hattie thought a minute. "You know, old April would probably be happier walking home if we milked her first. Is that okay?"

Inez turned hopeful eyes to the woman. "Can we, Enah? Please?"

The woman softened a bit and nodded.

Inez jumped up and down, her face widening in a gap-toothed smile. Hattie loved the special look little kids had when they were exchanging baby teeth for the permanent ones. She smiled warmly at the youngster.

"Come on then," she told Inez, "I'll introduce you to April, the runaway milk cow."

Together they followed Peter behind the shed where April stood munching hay in a small pen. Her eyes rolled, and she moved away, tossing her bony head at Eric. Holding the halter behind her back, Hattie walked up to her with the corn Peter had provided. After mooing at them all, the cow plunged her head into the bucket. Slipping the halter on securely,

Hattie tied it to a post and sat on the short stool Peter gave her. Picking up a clean bucket, she patted the cow's sweaty flank and turned to grin at Eric.

"Now, Mr. Siegen, this is what you do with a cow."

Eric cocked one eyebrow and tried to look indifferent, but Hattie noticed that he watched closely as she went to work. Soon thin streams of warm, white milk were hitting the pail. Inez kept drawing closer and closer until she could peek under Hattie's elbow.

"Will there be cream so we can make butter?" she asked.

"I hope so," said Hattie.

Even old Enah smiled a little as she watched with her arms folded. Hattie's discomfort had fled. She might not know about horn spoons, but she did know about milking cows and helping out a neighbor.

"How old are you?" she asked Inez.

"Almost eight."

"My cousin Pearl is seven. I think you two would have a good time together," said Hattie. Then she looked at Enah. "When Aunt Millie and her kids get well, you should come visit."

"They are sick?" the woman asked.

Hattie nodded. "Chicken pox. That's why we're here. My mama and grandmother . . ."

She didn't get the chance to finish her sentence. At the mention of chicken pox, something happened to the old woman. Her face tightened until the skin was white around her mouth, and her eyes flashed fire.

"Pox? You bring sickness to us?" She spun around faster than Hattie thought a woman of her age could move and grabbed a long hoe.

"Go away from here!" The low voice rose to a shriek as she waved the hoe menacingly. "Take your cow and your disease and leave us be!"

Nearly startled out of her stockings, Hattie jumped up. Eric hurried to untie April's head.

"We're sorry," he said, moving toward the gate. "But you see, we've already had chicken pox and can't get it—"

"Out!" screamed the woman, still swinging the hoe. Then, seeing the half-filled pail of milk, she knocked it spinning across the pen.

"No! My milk!" wailed Inez. Regina held her tightly as the foamy white milk soaked into the soil of the cow pen.

Hattie's head was reeling as they urged April into a trot across the yard. Eric called back, trying to explain. "There's really no danger, ma'am. My father's a doctor—"

Enah stood by her house, brandishing the hoe like a spear. Her calm face was livid and wet with tears.

"May God curse you if my children get sick!"

7

❖

Dirty Diapers and Dismal Dreams

Hatttie and Eric didn't look back until they reached the creek. When they paused there to rest, Hattie couldn't stop shaking.

"What's wrong with her, Eric? Nobody's *ever* talked to me that way!"

Eric shook his head. "She's scared, Hattie. I don't know—maybe she misunderstood and thought we meant smallpox."

"Well, she didn't have to get so angry. *We're* not sick."

"I know," he said. "I wish she had let us explain. But right now our problem is getting this old heifer home."

Hattie agreed, tapping April on the heel with a stick to persuade her to cross the creek. The cow picked up speed as they approached the farm and actually seemed glad to reach the barn.

"Do you want to try milking now?" Hattie asked.

Eric mopped the sweat from his face and grinned. "It would have saved a lot of trouble if I'd let you show me this morning. I'll get the feed bucket."

Soon April was happily munching as Hattie explained the finer points of milking. Eric was giving it a try when Mama burst through the barn door.

"Where on earth have you two been?" she demanded. "It's almost noon, and we're out of clean diapers for the baby. Hattie, I told you to start the wash this morning."

"The cow ran away, Mama. We've been chasing her all morning and . . ." Suddenly Hattie didn't want to talk about the Varga family, especially about Enah. Looking at Eric, she went on, "It's a long story. I'm sorry about the diapers. I'll get right to it."

Eric nodded. "It's my fault, Mrs. Marshall. I haven't spent much time with cows."

"I see," said Mama. "In that case, come have breakfast. You must be starving."

"Not really," said Eric before he caught Hattie's warning look. "I mean, yes, ma'am, we'll be right in."

When Mama left, he looked at Hattie. "Why don't you want to tell her about the breakfast we had with the Vargas?"

Hattie sighed. "I still feel awful about being run off like that, and I'm sorry we even met the Vargas. Old Enah probably won't sleep at night for worrying about the pox. And if we say anything around Aunt Millie's kids, they'll get excited about having someone new to play with. Clovis and Pearl would be down the creek hunting the Varga place before their spots were gone, while they're still contagious."

"I'm sure Enah would be thrilled," said Eric.

"Right. Maybe I'll tell Gramma though. She understands just about everything."

However, there was no time to talk with Gramma that day. After putting a huge washpot of water and lye soap on to boil, Hattie dealt with the diapers. Some were several days old, and she wanted to just burn them and make new ones; but that would be wasteful, which was one thing Gramma couldn't tolerate. So Hattie boiled and stirred, beating the diapers with a long, wooden paddle before lifting them into the rinse water. When they were finally free of soap, she hung them to dry in the hot sun.

Then it was time to start the other children's clothes. The boys' colorful shirts and the girls' calico dresses soon joined the cottony white diapers fluttering in the warm breeze. The work was going faster now, and Hattie's thoughts kept circling back to the morning's events. If only there was some way to explain to Mrs. Varga that she had nothing to worry about . . .

Hattie was so intent on that problem that she failed to notice another one—she had run out of clothesline. The three long cords strung between two trees were filled with flapping laundry, while a pot of bedsheets waited to be rinsed and hung.

"Phooey," said Hattie. "What am I supposed to

do now?" Leaving the clothes, she went to the barn and rummaged in Uncle Burl's assortment of stuff. It seemed that he had everything except clothes-line—old bottles, tools, horse harness, nails, even a barbed wire collection. Finally she spied a tangle of thin rope. If long enough, it was perfect.

Hattie took it to the tree where the other lines were tied. She climbed trees all the time at home, though usually not in a skirt. But no matter—she'd be through before anyone saw her.

Pulling the blue calico up around her knees, she found a foothold and hoisted herself up into a fork. The limb that Uncle Burl had tied the other clothes-lines to was farther out. He must have used a ladder, thought Hattie, but she dreaded the thought of find-ing it in the cluttered barn. Instead she scooted out onto the nearest limb and, tossing the rope over, reached to pull it around.

Just then she heard a noise at the barn and looked up, hoping it was Uncle Burl back from town. After all, this was really *his* job.

Instead, it was Eric. Seeing her skirt flapping in the tree, he stopped to stare.

"What are you looking at?" called Hattie. "Come help me."

Laying a large sack of peas in the shade, he ambled over. "Why are you hugging that tree?"

"Because I'm homesick," Hattie retorted. "Grab that end and tie this thing."

Eric obeyed, then reached up to help her down.

Not long ago she would have ignored him and climbed down by herself. But sometimes a little help was nice, if it was from the right person. She took his hands and jumped lightly to the ground. Unfortunately, her skirt stayed and wouldn't let go of the fork of the tree.

"Oh! Wait—"

"You're hung," said Eric, trying not to smile.

Flustered, keeping her back to the tree, Hattie snatched at the blue calico. It was hanging on to the bark, and when she pulled it free, a small piece of skirt was left behind.

"I have had . . . enough aggravation . . . for one day," she muttered.

"It's almost over," said Eric, picking up the rope. "Want me to tie this to the other tree?"

She nodded and went to rinse the sheets. Then Eric surprised her by wringing them out. Hattie was grateful, because her arms ached from the long afternoon of stirring and squeezing water from the heavy laundry. After dumping the last of the water, she looked at the clotheslines with satisfaction. The colorful clothes gave the yard a festive look. Feeling better, Hattie was about to thank Eric for his help when Pearl burst out the door. She was holding a basket.

"Look, Hattie!" she called. "Gramma said the new biddies have hatched, so I can go see 'em and pick up eggs. But just for a minute. Wanna come?"

Hattie had already seen the baby chicks and

was too tired to go anywhere. She shook her head as Pearl skipped across the yard. The sight reminded her of Inez. She wished that little girl could have kept the milk.

Though weary to the bone, Hattie couldn't rest that night, not with cows running through her dreams. There were crying children, too, but she wasn't sure if that part was dream or reality. Finally, sometime before daylight, little Michael's hungry wail erased any doubts. Stumbling to the kitchen, she warmed a bottle while Mama changed his diaper. As she tested the milk's temperature, Hattie thought about her dreams. She couldn't look at milk now without thinking about Inez.

"Thanks, honey," said Mama as Hattie gave her the bottle. "Go back to bed now. It's another hour before daylight."

Hattie trudged back to her pallet in the front room, but instead of lying down, she stared out the window. The white sheets hung ghostlike on the clothesline.

"There's still a piece of my skirt hanging in the tree, too," Hattie said to herself. "Guess I'd better fix that today. Mama will fuss if she sees it."

Something tugged in Hattie's mind, like trying to pull two ends of a rope together when they're too short. Something about milk and crying children and things hanging on trees. Then she knew . . .

Pulling her clothes on over her nightdress,

Hattie quietly slipped out the front door and dashed to the barn.

"Eric?" she called softly as she opened the creaky door.

There was no answer.

"Eric, wake up. I've got an idea."

"Who's there?" The hay rustled. "What's wrong?"

"It's me—Hattie. Nothing's wrong. I figured out what we can do about Enah and Inez."

Eric mumbled something she couldn't make out. Then he lit a lamp, and she could see him sitting on the bedroll he had spread in the hay. A few pieces of straw stuck out of his blond hair as he squinted in the light.

"This couldn't wait until morning?" he grumbled.

"No, 'cause we'll have to start early and get the chores done before we go back to the creek."

"We're not going back there," he said flatly.

"We have to," said Hattie. "We got those folks all upset, and I know how to fix it." She plunked down beside him. "We'll write them a letter."

"I doubt they get mail service, Hattie. What are you going to do—hang it around the cow's neck and send her back? Enah would probably shoot her."

Hattie sighed, trying to be patient. "No, we won't send April. We'll just go as far as the creek— where Peter found us. We can hang the letter on a tree and tie a jug of milk in the stream where it'll stay cool."

Eric rubbed his eyes. "What milk?"

"The milk for Inez. We have more than enough here. Once Enah understands that it doesn't carry chicken pox, maybe she'll keep it. We have to try."

"Hattie, you're asking for trouble. You should just leave those people alone."

Hattie hated to beg. Taking a deep breath, she looked her friend square in the eyes. "Eric, I've worried about this all night. If you won't help me, I'll do it by myself."

His sleepy face was a thundercloud. "Fine," he said crossly. "Just go away and let me sleep."

Stomping back to the house, Hattie remembered what Eric had said to Mama about it being hard to say no to her. Well, he certainly wasn't having trouble now.

8

Peace Offering

July 9, 1892

To the Varga family,

I am very sorry that we upset you about the chicken pox. It's true that my aunt and her kids are sick, and we came to help. But this isn't as dangerous as smallpox. Besides, Eric and I had chicken pox before, which means we can't catch it again. His father is a doctor, and my Gramma has taken care of sick folks all her life, so she's like a doctor—she even knows about Indian medicine.

When I asked Gramma about catching chicken pox, she said you have to be near the sick person or in their house. Eric, the cow, and I can't give it to you, so please don't worry. We have lots of milk, and I really want to share with Inez. Thanks for the breakfast.

Sincerely,
Hattie Marshall

Taking the nail she had brought, Hattie found a rock and hammered the letter to a large tree overlooking the creek. Then she tied one end of a rope around the trunk. At the other end a tightly sealed milk jug rested in the creek. The water would keep it cool, and the rope would keep it from drifting downstream.

Hattie looked around, wondering if anyone would find her message. The woods were quiet except for the chatter of a squirrel. Looking at the note, she sighed. It wasn't much, but it was all she could think to do.

She started up the trail. At the top of the hill a shadow moved. Hattie's grip tightened on her walking stick. Could it be Peter, or was it someone else?

"Who's there?" she called.

The shadow moved into the light, and the sun glinted off golden hair. It was Eric.

"What are you doing here?" Hattie demanded.

He shrugged. "Somebody has to keep you out of trouble."

"Well, thanks for spying on me," she snapped, brushing past him. "But I don't need your help."

"Did you see anyone?" he asked.

Hattie shook her head and trudged on, ignoring him. Eric followed in silence.

The walk back to Aunt Millie's seemed much shorter today without April, and soon they were in the back pasture. Uncle Burl waved when he saw them.

"Where have you two been?" he called.

Hattie hesitated, not knowing how much she should tell.

"Down the creek," she said truthfully.

"You should have taken a fishing pole," suggested Uncle Burl.

"That sounds good," said Eric. "Do you have a couple we could borrow one afternoon?"

"I reckon we could find some," said Uncle Burl, "for young'uns who've been as helpful as you two."

Hattie went on to the house. It was time to get back to being helpful.

The afternoon wore into evening as Hattie watched her young cousins, Ben and Billy. The combination of itching and little-boy energy made that a challenge. Though the Vargas occupied many of her thoughts, her immediate problem was how to keep the twins from killing each other.

First she tried hide-and-seek. The rambling house had all kinds of nooks and crannies, and Hattie found herself enjoying the lively game. That is, until Billy disappeared. Ben, who was "It," hunted until he got loud and frustrated, and Mama had to warn them about waking Aunt Millie.

Hattie, Clovis, and Pearl joined the search, looking everywhere. Though the twins were supposed to stay inside, Hattie went out to check the barn, the bushes, and under the house. A loud yell brought her running back inside.

It was Ben. Knowing his brother better than anyone, he had sneaked in to search Aunt Millie's room.

He found Billy beneath their mother's tall iron bed. When the angry Ben tried to pull him out, they got into a fight right under poor Aunt Millie, and Hattie had to drag them out wrestling and shrieking.

By the time they were separated, the twins had knocked Gramma's pine needle concoction all over the floor, rolled in it, and now smelled like soggy little squirrels. As they changed clothes, Hattie kept muttering to herself, thanking the Lord that she was the youngest in her family.

Next they tried shooting marbles in the living room. This worked for a while. Even little Winnie watched in fascinated silence as the colorful glass balls shot into each other across the hardwood floor. Then she decided to get into the game and popped Ben's green "tiger's eye" into her mouth. Hattie experienced a moment of panic as she sat on the furious Ben, trying to persuade Winnie to give the marble back before she swallowed it. Fortunately Clovis came in with a gingersnap about that time and convinced her to trade.

Things went on this way until bedtime, when Uncle Burl settled them down with a story and a tune on his violin. As Hattie escaped to the cool porch with peas to shell, she felt like her hair must be standing on end. A fishing trip sounded so good. But when would they have the time?

The next day was Sunday, and since the Cottons couldn't go to church because of the chicken pox, they had their own service. It was close to the real thing, with Uncle Burl leading music and Gramma telling Bible stories in her own special way. Most of the prayer time was about chicken pox and Aunt Millie getting well. When "church" was over, Mama and Gramma got busy fixing a proper Sunday dinner of fried chicken with rice and gravy. After Uncle Burl had eaten enough for three men, he quietly led Hattie and Eric to the barn.

"I found those fishing poles," he said. "And since it's too hot to do anything else, I thought you might like to try 'em."

Hattie nodded vigorously.

"All right then," said Burl as he pointed. "You can find worms under that catalpa tree. Don't be too late now, or your mama will be after me with a stick."

Hattie and Eric dug bait in record time. Then she got a jug of milk from the cooler, a large box outside the kitchen where food was stored in cold spring water to help keep it fresh.

"What's that for?" asked Eric.

Hattie shrugged. "Just in case . . ."

Following the creek, Eric soon found a deep spot with inviting shade. After baiting a hook, he got comfortable.

Hattie kept walking. "Play with fish if you like," she called back. "I have to see if someone found the note. Aren't you even curious?"

"Not really," he said. "Can't it wait?"

Leaving him behind, she hurried on, almost in a run. Climbing the hill, then making her way down, she spotted the tree with the clothesline tied to its trunk. The milk jug lay on the ground. It was empty. The letter was gone, too.

Hattie wanted to whoop and holler. Instead she hurried to untie the empty jug. Whoever found it must have poured the milk into another container. After anchoring the new jug in the creek, she stood and looked around. There was no message, no tracks, nothing to tell her who had come. But it didn't matter. Hattie hugged herself, feeling better than she had in days.

"Thank You, Lord," she whispered, "for helping me straighten things out. Maybe we can be friends with these folks yet."

She met Eric on the way back. His hair was all wet, and he looked refreshed.

"Did you jump in with the fish?" asked Hattie teasingly.

"Just for a minute," he said. "What did you find?"

"Someone got my note and the milk," she said excitedly. "Maybe Enah understands now. Oh, Eric, I want to go see them."

His face fell. "Hattie, don't start that again. One of the Vargas may have taken your letter, but you don't know if they believed it or want to be bothered."

"I'll take the chance," said Hattie, turning to go.

"No," warned Eric. "If you do, I'm telling your mother *everything*."

Hattie turned to glare at him. "Nothing I do is right with you. Everything's an argument."

"Then stop acting like one of the twins," he snapped. "You need a baby-sitter worse than they do."

The words stung as they soaked in, like strong medicine on an open cut. Hattie didn't know whether to cry or throw something at him.

Instead she shouted, "I wish you had stayed home!" Then she fled up the creek.

9

Regina

With hot tears blurring her vision, Hattie stumbled on through the woods toward the Vargas' cabin. Only once did she look back. Eric was nowhere in sight. *Good*, she thought. *I hope he goes back and stays there.*

Then, so suddenly that it surprised her, Hattie was in the clearing. She stepped back into the shadows of the trees and sat down to catch her breath. It was blistering mid-afternoon now, the heat giving the small, open field a wavy look. The family's horse and two cows sleepily swished flies in the shade of an oak tree, while a hog shuffled about in a pen behind the barn. There was no other movement. If the Vargas were like her folks, they would be resting inside until the heat of the day had passed.

Hattie mopped her face. Now that she was here, what should she do? The heat and the argument with Eric had weakened her resolve about this visit. *Wanting* to do something was one thing;

doing it was another. Resting her head on her knees, Hattie sat and prayed awhile—for wisdom, for courage, for Aunt Millie to get well soon—for lots of stuff. She also asked God how she could make things right with Eric. Fighting with her friend had left her knotted up inside. Somehow they had to stop their quarreling.

A door creaked, and Hattie raised her head. It was Regina going out to the well. The brown and white dog they called Deetsi was with her, and he turned to sniff in Hattie's direction. Words bubbled up inside Hattie, and she wanted to shout at Regina. Instead she found a pebble and skipped it across the yard. Deetsi growled at it suspiciously. Puzzled, the dark-haired girl looked around as Hattie quietly stepped from the trees and waved.

At first Regina looked startled. Then she waved back. Glancing at the cabin, she left the bucket of water and quietly walked to where Hattie waited at the clearing's edge. Deetsi got there first and started to bark in earnest.

"Shhh, boy," said Hattie. "It's okay. I'm a friend."

"Deetsi, be still," Regina ordered as she patted him gently. "Hello," she said to Hattie. "I'm surprised you came back."

Hattie let the dog sniff her fingers, then slowly rubbed his head. "Did you get my letter?" she asked.

Regina nodded. "Peter found it late yesterday. I read it for him."

"What did your grandmother say?"

"She is very . . ." Regina thought a moment. "She is very *protective* of us, Hattie. Some of her people died of smallpox, including my mother, so she worries about that. And it's hard for her to trust strangers."

"I'm sorry," said Hattie. "Did she keep the milk anyway?"

Regina's somber face brightened. "Inez begged her to. My little sister was very happy."

"That's great," said Hattie. At least one thing had turned out right today. "I left another jug at the creek if you want to go 'find' it."

Regina smiled. "Thanks. I'll do that. In fact, if you can wait a bit, I'll meet you there. We can talk better then."

"All right," said Hattie, almost too loudly. Then, with a lighter heart, she ambled back to the creek.

It was almost an hour before Regina appeared. Hattie had pulled off her shoes and stockings to wade in the creek. The water was cool and refreshing.

"I'm glad you waited," said Regina as she took off her shoes and apron and pulled the long red skirt up around her knees. Then she splashed out to join Hattie. "I go months without seeing anyone my age."

"How old are you anyhow?" asked Hattie.

"Fifteen last winter," said Regina.

"I'm not exactly your age then, but I'll be thirteen . . ." Hattie paused to think, and her eyes widened. "The day after tomorrow. We've been so busy that I lost track."

"Thirteen is close enough." Regina laughed. It was a pleasant sound, like the tinkling of the creek.

"Eric will be fifteen this fall," said Hattie.

"The boy you were with?"

Hattie nodded.

"He seemed very nice," Regina said thoughtfully. "I've never seen eyes that color. Is he your sweetheart?"

"No!" Hattie nearly choked. "We're just friends—at least sometimes, when we're not arguing. Right now I'm not sure what we are. I'm not old enough for that anyway."

"I almost wish that I weren't," said Regina. "It's funny at our house—Enah talks about my being old enough to think about marriage, but then she doesn't want me going anywhere that I'd meet young men. And Pa won't talk about it at all."

"My sister got engaged when she was sixteen," said Hattie. "She's seventeen now and got married last month. But I'm not interested," she quickly added.

Regina pushed up the sleeves on her dark calico blouse and tied her long hair back in order to splash her face. "I'd like to find someone special and have a family," she said. "But the only boys I know are my cousins over at Spanish Lake."

"Don't you go to school?" asked Hattie.

Regina's wet face wrinkled in a frown. "When I was small I did. Just long enough to learn reading. Pa said that someone in the family needed to know how."

"Didn't you like it?" asked Hattie.

"I liked learning new things, but the school is a long ways from here, and I always had to sit in the back of the room. Sometimes I got teased or called names," Regina said quietly, almost to herself. "One day I came home crying, and Enah said I didn't have to go back."

"What did your father say?"

"He was angry, too. And he respects Enah. So we stay home, and they teach us other things."

"I don't know why anyone would pick on you."

Regina looked at her sharply. "We're different, Hattie. Or haven't you noticed?"

Hattie thought a minute. The girl's golden brown skin and dark eyes told her that their backgrounds were probably very different. More than anything, the Vargas reminded her of the folks that came through town from Mexico and south Texas. Hattie wondered how they would be treated in *her* school.

"I haven't been much of anywhere," Hattie said finally. "At least not yet. When I grow up I hope to see all kinds of places and people. I expect they'll be different from what I'm used to, but that's the reason for going. Gramma says the world would be pretty dull if we were all the same, like stew made with nothing but potatoes."

Regina had to smile at that. "I guess you're

right." Sitting on a rock, she relaxed a little and kicked her bare feet in the water. "So how are the chicken pox people?"

"Well," said Hattie, "my Aunt Millie didn't take care of herself when she got sick, so she's the worst and has to stay in bed. But my cousins . . . they're plumb wild!"

As Hattie went on to tell of the twins' shenanigans, Regina laughed until she held her side. All too soon the sun dipped behind the treetops, and Hattie remembered that Uncle Burl had told her and Eric to be home early. She wondered if Eric had left the fishing hole, and if so, what he was telling Mama.

"I have to get back," she said. Pulling her feet out of the water, Hattie waved wrinkled toes in the air to dry before pulling on her stockings and shoes.

"Can you come again?" Regina asked.

"Sure," said Hattie as she picked up the milk jug. "Should I come here or to the house?"

"The house," Regina said thoughtfully. "I'll talk to Enah."

"Okay. Bye."

Hattie waved and took off up the creek. When she reached the deep part where she'd left Eric, her fishing pole was propped against a tree. Hattie shook her head as she grabbed it. She wondered if Eric had caught anything. But it didn't matter. She had found something worth far more—a new friend.

Mama met her on the porch. Her face was a storm cloud. "Where have you been?" she demanded.

"Down . . . at the . . . creek." Hattie stumbled over the words, then took a deep breath. Eric had not covered for her this time. She would have to tell Mama everything.

"When we were chasing the cow the other day, we met some folks living on the other side of the creek. They had caught April and fed her, and then they fed us, and they were real nice until we mentioned chicken pox. Then the grandmother got all scared and upset, so we left."

Hattie rushed on, "I wanted to explain that it was okay and share some milk 'cause their cow was sick. Today I saw the oldest girl, Regina, and we had a great visit. She's fifteen and doesn't have many friends. Don't be mad, Mama," she pleaded.

For a long moment Mama just stared. Then she sat back in the porch rocker and sighed. "Hattie Belle, what am I going to do with you?"

Hattie just shrugged and waited. She didn't figure Mama really wanted suggestions.

"Number one, you know better than to go home with strangers."

"But the cow . . ."

"Number two, you haven't been very honest with me."

Hattie studied her shoelaces. She couldn't argue with number two.

"And number three, we came here to help Millie and the kids. Running off and forgetting the time isn't very helpful."

Frowning, Hattie looked up at her mother. "Mama, I'm sorry for not telling you about the Vargas, but I've worked hard since we've been here."

"We *all* have," Mama said firmly.

Studying the dark circles under Mama's eyes, Hattie realized that she and Gramma hadn't stopped working since they arrived. That understanding made Hattie feel very childish.

"I won't leave the yard again without asking," she said. "I promise."

"You're not to leave at all," said Mama.

"But . . ."

"No buts. There has to be some punishment, Hattie, or you won't believe me when I tell you anything." With that, Mama rose and vanished into the house.

"I believe you," Hattie whispered. "But will Regina believe me anymore after I don't show up?"

10

Birthday Blues

Despite Hattie's resolve to make peace with Eric, it didn't happen the next day. He avoided the house as if *he* were the one afraid of chicken pox. And Hattie couldn't think of a single good reason to speak to him first. Maybe it would be better to leave things as they were.

Mama ordered a house cleaning, so Hattie was busy from dawn till dusk dusting, scrubbing floors, and keeping kids out of mischief. *When I turn thirteen things will have to be better than this*, she thought more than once that day.

Then, finally, her birthday came. As morning brightened the living room, Hattie got up from her pallet and stretched. Somehow she felt taller today. After all, now she was a teenager, like Sam, Rosalie, Eric, and Regina. No longer could they think of her as a little kid. As her cousins roused and dressed, they somehow looked younger to Hattie than the day before. They all giggled when Gramma stuck a candle in Hattie's scrambled eggs and everyone sang "Happy Birthday."

But the special feeling didn't last long. Mama had been up with Aunt Millie and the baby through the night and looked weary. When the breakfast dishes were washed, she pointed Hattie toward the laundry. Where had so many diapers come from?

Knowing it was no use to complain, Hattie started a fire under the washpot outside and hauled water for boiling. As she washed and stirred the dirty clothes, the July sun rose higher in the blue oven of a sky. How she longed to be home, where there would have been cake, homemade ice cream, and friends to share it with. Anything was better than spending your birthday being punished and having to wash other people's clothes.

The line was full of flapping laundry when Mama called Hattie in for dinner. As they munched thick ham sandwiches, Gramma looked at her kindly.

"What would you like for a birthday supper?" she asked.

"Fried fish," said Hattie, not looking at Mama.

"If they'd let me out of the house, I'd catch you a whopper," said Clovis.

"Me, too," Ben chimed in.

"I'd catch the biggest," bragged Billy.

"Then we'd have quite a fish fry," Hattie said gratefully.

Eric said nothing.

Mama frowned as she tried to prod Winnie's

mouth open for another bite. Hattie decided to drop the subject of fishing. Generally when Mama punished you, she wouldn't let you off the hook.

As the cousins went off for their naps and Hattie cleared the table, Mama stopped and folded her arms.

"Hattie, I've been thinking. It's a sad thing not to have any fun on your birthday, though I'm not sure you've learned a lesson from your punishment yet."

"Oh, but I have, Mama. I promise not to go off again without telling you where."

"Now that you're a teenager, I do expect you to act more responsibly," Mama said sternly.

"I will," Hattie promised. "You'll see."

Mama grunted. "All right then . . . I'm going to make an exception since this is an exceptional birthday. You and Eric can go catch some fresh fish for supper, but I want you back by 5 o'clock *sharp*. Understand?"

Hattie wanted to shout for joy. Then she had another thought. "Can I go see Regina, too? I told her I'd come back."

Mama's frown deepened. "Just long enough to fetch Millie's milk jug. That is, if Eric doesn't mind going there."

For the first time, Hattie looked at him.

He looked over at Mama. "Whatever you say, Mrs. Marshall," he said without emotion.

Hattie grabbed Mama and hugged her. "All right!"

"How will the babies get to sleep with your noise?" Mama said crossly. "Get going now."

Hattie didn't give Mama a chance to change her mind. She hurried out the door and gathered the fishing gear. Taking a pole, Eric marched off across the pasture without a word. Hattie sighed and followed him in silence to the creek. It was a twenty-minute walk to the pool where he had fished before. As Eric baited his hook, Hattie fidgeted.

"I'd like to see Regina first," she finally said.

"I thought we came to catch supper."

She took a deep breath, determined not to start an argument. "I know that. But if we go there first, maybe the kids can come back and fish with us. Wouldn't you like that?"

He thought a minute. "All right. But if we're not welcome this time, that's the end of it. Agreed?"

Hattie nodded and hurried up the creek. She slowed down as they neared the cabin, then peeked out from the trees. Enah was throwing out scraps for the chickens, while Peter and his father worked in the shed. The girls were hoeing in the cornfield.

Hattie timidly stepped from the shadows and walked up to the woman. Enah froze when she saw Hattie, looking her up and down with those dark, piercing eyes.

"What do you want here?" she asked.

Hattie opened her mouth, but nothing came out. She cleared her throat and tried again. "Eric and I came to catch some fish for supper. I was hoping your kids could come, too."

"I think fish for supper sounds fine," said a deep voice.

Hattie didn't realize that Lou Varga had joined them.

"The girls have worked hard this morning, and Peter can help me work on the canoe later," said their father.

Enah didn't answer him. Instead she spoke to Hattie. "How are your relatives? Are they well?"

"Not yet," said Hattie. "The chicken pox take awhile, but Gramma says they'll be fine soon."

"Your grandmother—she is a medicine woman?"

That sounded so odd that Hattie almost laughed, then thought better of it. "Yes, ma'am, I guess you could say that."

Enah cocked her head. "What does she do when your stomach hurts?" she asked.

Hattie had to think a minute. She hadn't expected a test.

"Well, she makes a tea with willow bark. It tastes awful, but it usually helps. Since she hurt her hip last fall, it's hard for her to find plants in the woods. Now she sends me."

"What plants?"

"Dogwood and persimmon root . . . and yaupon leaves."

This seemed to satisfy Enah, who nodded. "A true medicine woman wouldn't let you come if there was danger of spreading sickness. My children can go fishing if they want."

The girls, who had been eavesdropping, dropped their hoes. Regina ran to the cabin, returning with Aunt Millie's milk jug and a small leather parcel that she handed to Hattie.

"For your birthday," she said shyly.

Hattie's mouth fell open in surprise as she untied the leather thongs. Inside lay an object about the size of her hand and shaped like a butterfly. It was stiff and covered with heavy black cloth. Tiny white beads were sewn in a design she didn't recognize, and four colorful ribbons hung with tiny mussel shells were attached at the end. Another ribbon was tied securely around the middle with the ends dangling on the back side.

Hattie hated to ask what the object was, but her confusion must have shown.

Regina smiled and pointed to the back of Enah's head, where her long pewter hair was wrapped in a bun. A similar piece of handwork was fastened there with tiny pieces of silver attached.

"It's a *dushta*," said Regina. "Now that you're older, you'll be putting your hair up sometimes. All the women in our family wear them."

"Oh," said Hattie. "Thank you. It's very pretty. Maybe you can help me fix it later."

Regina nodded, and together they followed the boys back up the creek. Peter knew of another good fishing spot, a sunlit pool fed by the creek. Soon they were baited and trying to wait quietly for a bite. It wasn't easy with so much to talk about. Hattie enjoyed telling Regina and Inez about her family and friends back home.

"Have you ever been to Texas?" she asked the girls.

"We've never been anywhere," grumbled Inez.

"That's not true," said Regina. "We've been to Natchitoches and Robeline to trade, and to Spanish Lake to see our mother's people."

"Then Enah is your father's mother?" asked Hattie.

Regina nodded.

"Where are they from?"

"Here. This land has always belonged to Enah's family."

"But everyone had to come from somewhere," said Hattie. "I thought maybe your folks were from Mexico."

Regina shook her head. "I don't know. At least Enah has never said that. She doesn't like talking about the past, so we don't ask questions. Maybe it's painful since she lost so much family to sickness. Where did your people come from?"

Hattie thought a minute. "I guess England to start with. My teacher says that years ago the king there wouldn't let folks live or worship God like they wanted, so they packed up and came to America. There was plenty of land, and though they had hard times, they were free to govern themselves."

"So you're English," said Regina.

"Oh no, I'm American," laughed Hattie. "That

was a long time ago. Some more of our folks came from Ireland 'cause they were so poor. But that was way back. Their kids had kids and kept moving west. Gramma's family came to Texas when she was small and the neighbors were Indians. They were pioneers," Hattie said proudly.

"I see." Regina was thoughtful, hardly noticing when a fish tightened her line.

"Look! You've got one!" cried Peter.

As Regina pulled back, the fish floundered; it was a big one. The boys dropped their poles to help, and after a slippery wet tussle the healthy-looking bass was landed.

"It's beautiful," said Eric, carefully taking out the hook and handing Regina her catch. He always got excited about bass. "You're quite a fisherman."

"Thank you," said a beaming Regina. Or was she blushing?

"What kind of hook is this, anyway?" he asked.

"Pa makes them from nails."

"That's a good idea." Eric carefully examined the curved metal with the square head. Then he looked at the girl, as if for the first time. "Your father's making a boat too, isn't he?"

Regina nodded. "A dugout canoe. He covered part of a cypress log with wet mud, then burned out the center. Now he . . ."

"Now *I'm* helping him clean it and smooth it out," interrupted Peter. "It's man's work."

Regina gave her brother a sideways look and

propped her pole against a tree. "Want me to fix your hair now?" she asked Hattie.

Hattie agreed, and they worked together until her long hair was wrapped in a tight bun and fastened to the back of her head. Regina tied on the *dushta* and stood back with a satisfied smile.

Hattie carefully felt the back of her head and studied her reflection in the water. The few times Mama had put her hair up always made her look older. Today she didn't mind.

"Thanks," said Hattie. "I don't know how you did that without pins."

"Practice," said Regina. "You have very nice hair."

"It covers a very hard head," commented Eric.

Hattie made a face at him but held her tongue.

"Now fix mine." Inez, who was already tired of fishing, plunked herself down in front of Regina.

The older girl sighed and deftly undid her little sister's long braids. Then, as Inez happily chatted with Hattie, Regina pulled a thin reed from the water, snapped it into two short pieces, and braided the thick black hair around them. Hattie watched, trying not to laugh and spoil Regina's joke. When Hattie could bear it no longer, she turned away and noticed Eric staring at her.

"Have a look," Regina said proudly when she finished.

Inez knelt down to admire herself in the pool. Both braids stuck out stiff and straight behind her head.

"Agh!" the eight-year-old shrieked. "What have you done to me?"

"Will you be quiet? You're scarin' the fish," said Peter. Then he saw what Regina had done and shook with laughter.

Eric, who rarely laughed at anything, grinned at them.

"You never know," he said. "That could become New York's latest fashion."

Regina smiled at him, and her dark, thick-lashed eyes sparkled. It occurred to Hattie that Regina was very pretty when she smiled. She wondered if Eric had noticed that.

Inez stopped yelling and pulling at her braids. Taking a second peek in the water, she giggled. "Do you think Pa would like it?" she asked.

"He'll love it," Hattie promised. "Leave it up till you get home."

Several fish later Eric looked at his pocket watch and announced that it was 4:30.

"Time for us to get back or I'll be in trouble again," said Hattie. "Thanks for the . . ."

"*Dushta*," said Regina. "You're welcome." She looked at Eric. "I hope you both can come back."

"So do I," said Hattie.

"We'll be back," Eric said confidently.

Hattie wondered what had changed his mind.

11

❖

The Visit

"Mama, look what Regina gave me," called Hattie as she came into the house. She had walked carefully all the way back, trying not to mess up her bun.

"Where?" asked Mama.

Hattie turned to show her. "It's a *dushta*."

"How unusual." Mama studied the beaded hairpiece. "It's very nice, Hattie. Now, do we have enough fish for supper?"

"Yes, ma'am. Eric's cleaning them. I'm going to show Gramma."

She found Gramma doctoring Winnie's chicken pox. The spots were beginning to dry up now, and the child's fever was gone, so she was in a better mood.

"Happy birfday to Hattie," she sang.

"Thanks, Winnie. See what my friend gave me?"

Winnie fingered the small, colorful ribbons while Gramma examined the careful beadwork. "Who made this?" asked Gramma.

"Regina—the girl I told you about."

Gramma was silent, and her face got all creased up like she was thinking hard.

"What's the matter?" asked Hattie.

"Nothing," said Gramma. "I've seen a hairpiece like this before, but I can't remember where. It was a long time ago."

Hattie went to show it to Pearl.

The long day was finally drawing to a close as they sat down to fried fish, potatoes, hush puppies, and birthday cake. Uncle Burl found a ripe watermelon in his patch, and Aunt Millie even got out of bed to join them. Hattie ate until she thought she would explode.

Then came the presents. Mama had brought along a new dress she was working on, though she still hadn't found time to finish it. Gramma gave Hattie a small box wrapped in red tissue paper. Hattie couldn't imagine what it was.

She opened it carefully.

"Gramma! It's beautiful."

The cousins crowded around to see. Inside the tiny box lay a thin gold band with a sparkling red stone.

"It's a ruby," said Gramma, "your birthstone."

"Oh, Gramma, it's so beautiful," said Hattie, slipping the ring on each of her fingers until she found the one that fit. Then she wrapped Gramma in a bear hug. "I'll keep it forever," she said.

Gramma nodded with satisfaction.

Next Uncle Burl brought out a wooden cabinet about a foot square and divided into three narrow shelves. The front was open and bordered by delicate carving.

"This is from Millie and me," he said. "You can hang it in your room. We know you girls like a place for your what-nots."

"It's great, Uncle Burl." Hattie hugged him, too. "I can't wait to put it up."

Pearl then presented Hattie with a bouquet of flowers she had slipped outside to pick. The twins had drawn pictures of Fritter. Winnie also had artwork—a funny shape with red spots.

"It's me wif chicken pox," she said, and everyone laughed appprovingly.

Then Clovis handed Hattie a small tin horse with a cowboy on his back. "It's to remind you of Sam," he said. "You can put it on your shelf."

Hattie couldn't speak for a moment. Thinking about Sam often did that to her. Instead she hugged Clovis and gave his head a kiss as his round, spotted face turned pink.

When the party was over and Hattie went to throw out the watermelon rinds, she found Eric waiting on the porch. His hands were stuffed in his pockets, and his face looked somber.

"I'm sorry I don't have a present for you," he said. "We left home in such a hurry that I didn't think about it."

Hattie shrugged, pretending it didn't matter. "I

105

didn't expect one," she said. She never knew what to expect from him anymore anyway.

Eric fidgeted a minute. "So how do you like being thirteen?"

"I don't know yet," she said. "But the day certainly ended better than it started."

"That's true," said Eric. "I'm glad we went back to the Vargas'. I don't like being on bad terms with people any more than you do, but I didn't see a way to fix it. You did real well, Hattie."

Something flickered inside her, giving her a warm glow. "Thanks," she said as she sauntered into the house.

The next few days passed in a slow blur of laundry, canning, and entertaining children. Hattie found that "playing school" kept most of them occupied for the longest periods of time. Being the teacher also made her feel quite grown-up, especially when Eric stopped by to listen to her "class." The cousins enjoyed being read to, so she searched through the family's books and Gramma's Bible for stories that would hold their interest. Even the rambunctious twins sat wide-eyed as she read about David and Goliath one day and Tom Sawyer the next.

Finally Mama declared that Hattie's punishment was over and she was free to visit the Vargas when her chores were done. This time Eric went along without being asked.

All of the family except Enah seemed pleased to see them. She went on with her cooking as the girls showed off their garden patch. Hattie had never seen such an assortment of squash, gourds, corn, and pumpkins. Many of the long-necked gourds had been dried and cleaned to use as dippers, or were hung from trees as birdhouses. Hattie watched in delight as a tiny wren fed her babies in a gourd-house hanging from the back porch.

Then they met the Varga livestock, including a huge, spotted sow and the cow that would soon have a calf. At the edge of the clearing, Peter was introducing Eric to a pet raccoon perched on his shoulders. It chattered saucily at Deetsi, who barked but kept his distance. However, as the girls drew near, the masked critter decided the tree was safer and scrambled to a limb.

"Since Enah chased him from the corncrib with a hoe, he doesn't trust anyone in a skirt," laughed Regina.

"Oot, come down," coaxed Peter.

The coon just chattered.

"Oot?" asked Hattie.

"That's his name," said Peter.

"What's it mean?"

"I don't know. It's what Enah calls him," Peter explained. "She's usually mad and looks funny when she says it, but that's what I named him."

"If you really want to make friends with Oot, you could wear overalls," Hattie told Regina. "Maybe he'd think you were a boy."

"I don't believe that would fool even a raccoon," Eric commented as if to himself.

Hattie just looked at him.

"Oh no," said Regina, "Inez and I never wear men's clothes. Enah would have a fit."

Eric changed the subject. "How's the boat coming along?"

"Come on," said Peter. "I'll show you."

The cypress log was almost hollow now, and the ends were growing more defined.

"When this is finished, Pa and I will do some serious fishing on the lake," Peter bragged.

About that time Enah called them to the house for dinner. Hattie and Eric hesitated, but she waved them on.

"There is plenty," she said. "You come, too."

Glad that the woman was softening toward them, Hattie followed the others inside. A spicy smell filled the cabin. As they sat down, she saw the reason. From a large pot over the fire Enah was scooping up small rolls of dripping corn shucks.

"Tamales?" asked Eric.

Enah nodded.

"My mother has tried to make these," he said, "but we couldn't eat them. It was her first try with Mexican food, and she used too much jalapeño."

"They are not Mexican," said Enah, turning to dip from another pot.

"Oh?" said Eric, waiting for an explanation.

She gave him none, instead filling a plate with steaming boiled corn on the cob. Regina brought in a bowl of pale yellow butter from the well.

"There was enough cream on the milk you brought to make this," she said. "We've enjoyed it."

"I'm glad," said Hattie between mouthfuls. "I can bring some more if you want it."

"Oh, yes," said Inez.

Inez's father gave her a stern look. "Isn't the milk from your uncle's cow?" he asked Hattie.

"Yes, sir, but he doesn't mind."

"Then I'll send him something in exchange for it," Lou said thoughtfully. "Does he grow squash?"

"Only the yellow crookneck," said Eric. He had spent enough time in the garden to know.

"Then we'll send something different," said Lou.

Hattie shrugged. She knew it wasn't necessary, but her father would probably have said the same thing.

When they had finished and were about to leave, Lou appeared with a heavy basket of green, acorn-shaped squash, small melons, and fat-bottomed gourds. "Can you carry this?" he asked.

"Sure," said Eric, grasping both ends.

Hattie was about to take one side, but the look on Eric's face was the one she'd seen on boys when they were showing off a bit. That wasn't typical of

Eric, but she left him alone. By the time they had said goodbye and crossed the creek, he was puffing hard.

"Would you like some help now?" she asked.

Eric sat the basket down and wiped his face. "This must weigh forty pounds," he panted.

"Oh, but I'm sure Regina was impressed by your muscles," Hattie said sarcastically.

"What are you talking about?"

"I'm not blind," she said. "She's always making eyes at you."

"You're imagining things," he mumbled.

Hattie couldn't tell if he was blushing or if it was just the heat. "It's lonesome out here, and she thinks you're really nice," said Hattie. "I didn't imagine that—she told me."

Eric grunted and grabbed his end of the basket. "Well, she's nice, too."

Hattie lifted the other side of the basket. It *was* heavy.

"Do you think Regina's pretty?" Hattie asked. She held her breath, waiting for the answer.

Eric pondered a minute, then turned those indigo eyes to bore into hers. "Does it really matter to you what I think?"

It was Hattie's turn to blush. "Not in the least," she said as she marched on toward the house.

12

Medicine Woman

Two days later Hattie and Eric went back to the Vargas' again. It was just past noon, with a blistering sun and still air that turned the cotton field's dew into a steam bath. When Uncle Burl had told them to find something cooler to do, they'd headed for the creek, promising to hoe the cotton that evening.

Today Eric carried the basket, lighter now, holding only another jug of April's milk. Uncle Burl had never met his quiet neighbors, but he was fascinated with the squash and small melons they had shared.

Deetsi greeted Hattie and Eric as they entered the clearing. Hattie expected to find the Varga clan resting in the house. Instead Inez waved from the garden, where she was helping Enah and her father. Peter called them over to the shade of a tree where he and Regina were scraping a fresh deerskin.

"Look what got into the garden last night," said Peter. "This buck and a couple of does made a mess of it. Enah's still upset about her plants. She's been

111

out there since daylight trying to fix 'em. Pa and I followed the tracks to the creek. We were so quiet, they never knew we were there. I got the buck with one shot," Peter said proudly.

"I'm impressed," said Eric as he counted the tips on the buck's horns. The eight-pointed rack had been cut away and now lay on the ground beside the stretched hide.

"There will be no living with Peter now," Regina said with a smile that lingered as she looked toward Eric.

"Where was Deetsi while the deer were eating the garden?" asked Hattie.

"Who knows?" said Regina. "Our brave watchdog was off chasing a rabbit or some other dangerous varmint."

Peter rubbed the dog's shaggy head. "That's all right. Old Deet knew I wanted to shoot a deer." Deetsi sniffed and growled at the deerskin as if that was exactly what he had in mind.

Hattie watched as they worked, scraping the hide to clean and soften it. She had seen Sam and Papa do the same many times. But there was one difference.

"What's that thing you're scraping with?" she asked.

Regina held up a piece of dark blue glass the size of a small child's palm. One edge was rolled and smooth, while the other half was slightly curved and chipped with ragged edges.

"A scraper," Regina said. "We make them from old bottles. For some chores they work better than a knife."

Hattie took the scraper and examined it closely. One edge nicked her finger. "This is really sharp," she said. "It's a good idea though. Papa is always having to sharpen his knives."

"I'll give you one to take home to Texas," said Regina. "When will that be anyway?"

Hattie looked at Eric, who shrugged. "The chicken pox are healing," she said, "and my aunt's pneumonia is better. But she won't be strong enough to cook or wash clothes or chase kids for a while yet. My Uncle Burl hopes we'll stay till Christmas," laughed Hattie.

"I wish you could," Regina said earnestly.

Hattie didn't know how to answer that. Though she missed home, it would be hard to say goodbye. Apparently Eric didn't know what to say either, so he knelt down to examine Peter's work.

"I think you'd really like my cousins," Hattie said finally. "Maybe you can visit when everyone is well."

"Maybe," answered Regina, going back to her scraping.

"We'll probably come again next year," Hattie offered, trying to sound cheerful. "Mama and Aunt Millie just have to see each other . . ."

She was interrupted by a shout. The four of them jumped and looked toward the garden. At first Hattie could only see Inez jumping and waving.

Then Lou Varga shouted again, his voice loud and urgent. He was kneeling over something . . . or was it someone?

"Enah!" Regina screamed.

Deerlike, she rose up and flew across the yard before Hattie could open her mouth. Peter bounded after her. Hattie looked at Eric, and they, too, ran for the garden.

They found Lou kneeling beside his mother, shielding her from the hot sun and talking quietly. Enah's face was pouring with sweat as she clutched her chest and gasped for breath.

Inez jumped up and down, her voice rising in a hysterical shriek. "Get up, Enah! Get up!" cried the child. "What's wrong with her?"

Regina knelt, too, and gripped Enah's gnarled hand. "What happened? What can we do?" she cried.

Lou shook his head and motioned for them to be quiet.

"I guess the heat is too much for her. Let's get her inside where it's cooler. Regina, get a blanket," he ordered.

"Mr. Varga," Eric said quietly, "when my father treats someone with a seizure, he sits them up a bit. It helps them breathe and makes the blood flow better."

Lou reached behind Enah's shoulders and gently lifted her. "Enah, can you hear me? Is this better?" he said softly.

The woman's leathery face was twisted in pain, and her eyes were shut tight, but she nodded.

"What else does your father do?" asked Lou.

Eric thought a second. "He keeps the patient comfortable and has medicines that help some-times."

Regina appeared with a large blanket, which they spread on the ground beside Enah.

"We're going to take you in the house now," said Lou.

Together they lifted her onto the blanket. Enah clutched her chest with both hands, and her breath came in short gasps as they carried her inside. While Regina fetched a towel and water, Lou looked at Hattie.

"You said that your grandmother is a medicine woman?"

Hattie nodded. The name wasn't funny now.

"There's nothing more I can do for Enah," Lou went on. "I have no medicine. Do you think your grandmother can help?"

"I don't know," she said honestly. "But if Gramma were here, she'd try. Do you want me to get her?"

Lou nodded. "If she'll come."

"Sure, she will," said Hattie. She turned toward the door. "I'll . . . I'll hurry."

They left Lou trying to talk with Enah as the girls bathed her face and arms with the cool water. Hattie's heart ached for them. All they could do was wait and pray for their loved one.

Hattie did some praying herself as she and Eric

ran toward Aunt Millie's. It had only been months since Gramma had fallen on icy steps and Sam had searched the county for Doc Siegen. That had been one of the longest days of Hattie's life, with Gramma in such pain, and Hattie not knowing if she'd recover. Hattie hated the scared, helpless feeling that had clawed at her insides then and must be doing the same to Regina now.

Dear Lord, please help Enah to hang on. I know she doesn't like me much, but it doesn't matter. Her family needs her. Please help them to be brave, and help Gramma to know what to do.

The minutes crawled as they took the quickest paths through the woods and along the creek. Eric led the way, and though the long skirt slowed her down, Hattie was determined to keep up with him. Pulling the calico up around her knees, she plunged through the shallow water and struggled up the bank. Then an awful thought occurred.

"Eric," she panted, "Gramma can't make it to the Vargas' this way!"

He turned to stare at her. "You're right. We'll have to find another way to get back. Can she ride a horse?"

"She hasn't in years," said Hattie. "Do you think we could get there in a wagon?"

Eric shook his head. "I'm not sure. Maybe your uncle will know."

They hurried on. The woods grew thick again, and undergrowth grabbed hold of Hattie's skirt, tripping her as they climbed a sharp rise. Then her lungs began to burn, and pain stabbed her side. As she held her hand over her ribs, Eric glanced back.

"Are you okay?"

Hattie nodded but was too out of breath to speak. Instead she waved him on. He hesitated, then disappeared over the hill.

Though Hattie reached the house only minutes behind Eric, Gramma was already gathering her things. Eric and Uncle Burl stood on the porch, trying to figure a way to take her to the Vargas' by wagon.

"You say it's down the creek and straight through there?" Uncle Burl pointed with one hand and scratched his head with the other. "There's an old wagon trail that cuts off the main road as you head north. I've never had cause to go that way."

"We have to try, Uncle Burl," said Hattie.

"I know, girl," he said. "We asked you all to come a lot further than that to help us. Guess I'd better hitch the team."

Eric and Uncle Burl disappeared into the barn as Hattie told Gramma everything she knew about Enah's condition.

Gramma shook her head. "It sounds like angina. I can't fix everything, honey, but we'll do what we can."

"I knew you would, Gramma." Hattie wrapped her in a grateful hug as a tear escaped. "I just keep remembering how it felt when you were hurt."

Gramma patted her shoulder. "Well, I'm a tough old bird, and your friend sounds like one, too. Fetch my sassafras now, and we'll get going."

Soon they were on the way in Uncle Burl's buckboard—first to the main road, then off in a direction Hattie had never been. Eric pulled out his pocket watch, looked at her, and shook his head. Precious time was being lost going this long way around, but it couldn't be helped.

What if they were too late? The thought pulled like a heavy weight on Hattie's heart.

After what seemed like hours, Uncle Burl stopped at a break in the forest. The strip of bare red earth winding through the trees looked more like a deer path than a road.

"This is it," said Uncle Burl. "I don't know what's back here, but it takes us the way you showed me."

Hattie looked at Eric, who nodded. "Let's try it," she said.

The main road had been bumpy, but Hattie felt sure this one would shake her insides loose. Trying to see ahead, she had to duck as drooping limbs snatched her hair. Gramma held tight to her bonnet with one hand and the buckboard with the other.

The wagon leaned as the trail skirted around a steep hill and turned upward. *Surely*, Hattie thought, *we must be getting close. Please, Lord, let this be the right way.*

Slowly they climbed. The sun was dipping below the treetops now. It had been over two hours since Enah's attack. Then, from somewhere in the forest, a dog barked. "It must be Deetsi!" Hattie hollered. There weren't any other dogs out this way.

Eric saw the cabin first and shouted victoriously. Hattie's stomach tightened as they bounced into the clearing and watched for someone to come out. When Uncle Burl stopped the mule, a teenaged girl rushed out of the cabin. It was Regina. Her face was streaked with tears.

13

The Secret

Were they too late? Hattie's heart skipped a beat as she jumped from the wagon and ran to Regina. The sobbing girl grabbed her friend and held her tight.

"Regina, I'm sorry it took so long," Hattie tried to explain. "How is . . . how is Enah?"

Shaking her head, Regina tried to speak. "She passed out. . . . She's talking out of her head. Hattie, we don't know what to do."

Hattie patted the girl's trembling shoulders. "I know how you feel," she whispered. "But Gramma's here. It'll be okay."

The others had caught up with them now. Eric was helping Gramma, and Uncle Burl was carrying her bag. Regina let go of Hattie and tried to greet Gramma, but instead of words there were only more tears.

Then, so quickly that Hattie could only stand there with her mouth open, Regina wrapped her arms around Eric. He held tight as she clung to him, crying pitifully.

Seeing the look on Hattie's face, Gramma pulled her inside. "Where's the patient?" Gramma asked firmly.

Hattie just stared. For the moment she had forgotten Enah and their reason for being there. All she could think about was Eric and Regina.

Lou Varga's deep voice woke her up. "Thank you for coming," he said.

They entered the cabin and turned to the corner where Enah was lying. Inez sat curled like a cat at her feet. Peter was not anywhere inside. Lou introduced himself to Gramma and gave her his chair. Enah still lay half-propped on her narrow bed. Her eyes were closed.

"She's been talking a lot, but it's mostly to herself," said Lou. "We can't make much sense of it."

Gramma took Enah's stout hand in her thin one and gently squeezed the brown arm to feel the blood pulsing through the old woman's veins.

"Howdy," Gramma said quietly. "I'm Anna Marshall, Hattie's grandma. Can you hear me?"

Taking a deep, labored breath, Enah nodded and opened her eyes to stare at Gramma.

"Can you tell me how you feel?" Gramma asked.

In low, halting words Enah told Gramma about the deer in her garden, the heat, and the pain that had gripped her chest as if it meant to squeeze the life out of her. Then the weary eyes closed, and her words drifted into jumbled sounds that Hattie couldn't understand.

As Gramma listened, Inez rose to wrap a small arm around Hattie's waist. Hattie hardly noticed. Looking at the door, her mind churned. There was no reason to be upset, she told herself. Eric was Regina's friend, just as Hattie was; and friends were meant to comfort each other. But no amount of reasoning could untie the knot growing in her stomach. It was jealousy, mean and green, as Papa would say. Hattie hated the feeling but also didn't want to let it go.

Then the door swung open, and *they* came in, along with Peter. Regina's face was red, but she had stopped crying and quietly sat near Enah. Eric stood by Uncle Burl, avoiding Hattie's eyes.

"You menfolk and the little one go outside now," Gramma ordered. "I need to examine the patient. Hattie, I want you to stay. Young lady," she pointed to Regina, "you can put some water on to boil."

When the others had left, Gramma looked and listened and poked Enah until Hattie expected Enah to flash those dark eyes and tell Regina to get her hoe. Instead she just lay there, limp as an old blanket, mumbling something about "don't tell the children."

Enah must be really sick, thought Hattie, *or she'd never let a stranger get so personal*. Maybe it was the caring of one old woman for another that had softened her heart. Hattie tried to pay attention, to think about something—*anything*—besides Eric and Regina.

Finally Gramma was finished. Taking the hot water Regina brought, she mixed up a cup of sassafras tea. As she spooned it into her patient's mouth, Gramma talked.

"You've got what we call angina back home," she told Enah. "Sometimes it brings on seizures like you've had. No one seems to know if it's the lungs not getting air or the heart growing weak. Those book-learned doctors have pills that help some folks, but I use sassafras tea. It's good for the blood; it purifies and thins it."

Swallowing the tea, Enah nodded.

"Do you know where to find the root?" Gramma asked.

Enah nodded again.

"It seems we sort of went to the same school," said Gramma, spooning more of the tea into her patient's mouth.

"The Good Lord's given you a warning," Gramma went on. "He's telling you that it's time to slow down. Some folks don't make it through a seizure like you had. You'll need to stay in bed awhile, then start back slow. And don't be working in the heat of the day, not even if a whole herd of deer comes through the garden."

Enah frowned. "We have to eat," she mumbled.

"I know it's hard to slow down when you've

worked all your life," said Gramma. "But if you don't take care, another seizure could be your last."

Enah leaned back and closed her eyes, refusing to take more tea. "Then I am useless," she whispered. "I go to *Kee-wut-hi-u*."

"There she goes again," Regina said anxiously, "talking gibberish."

Gramma said nothing. Instead she took Enah's hand, bowed her head, and spent a long time in prayer. Hattie held her breath, marveling at how different and yet how alike the two women were. It was a holy moment of kinship.

When Gramma finished, Enah had apparently dozed off, for her breathing was deeper. Gramma went to the table and poured hot water for more tea. While it steeped, she sniffed the half-eaten tamales someone had left, then turned to study Regina with a funny, puzzled frown.

"You're wearing a hairpiece like the one you gave Hattie," she said to the girl. "It's very pretty."

"Thank you," Regina said quietly.

Gramma stirred the tea. "Where do you folks come from anyway?"

"We've always lived here," said Regina. "It's Enah's land."

Gramma nodded thoughtfully. Then she knelt by the cookfire. A crock of fresh corn and beans slowly bubbled, filling the cabin with a sweet aroma. Beside it was a long horn spoon that Gramma used to stir and taste the corn. Fresh corncobs still lay there beside a scraper. Regina gathered them, looking embarrassed.

"I was working on this when Peter came home with the deer," she mumbled. "I should have cleaned the mess."

Gramma didn't seem to hear. Instead she picked up the scraper. It was made of broken green glass, smooth on one side and carefully chipped into a cutting tool on the other, just like the one Regina had shown Hattie. Light shone in Gramma's eyes as she went to sit by Enah again, waiting quietly until she awoke. As the woman stirred, Gramma offered her more tea.

"You're wrong about being useless," Gramma said softly. "All children need their *enah*, even if she can't do everything she used to."

The dark eyes bored into Gramma's.

"I haven't seen one of these since I was a little girl," Gramma said, turning the scraper over in her hand. "There were some folks that lived in the hills near our place . . ."

"Enough," Enah said with more strength than Hattie thought she possessed. She tried to raise up. "Regina, go outside!"

Regina stared at her. Then, with a mystified look, she left. Hattie hesitated, not knowing what to do.

Enah pointed a finger at her, then looked at Gramma. "You'll tell her anyway?" she asked. Her voice had a bitter edge.

"We don't have many secrets in our house," said Gramma.

Enah shook her head sadly. "There are too many in ours. They weigh on my heart and make it weak."

"Your children don't know they're Indian?"

Gramma's question hung like smoke in the air. Enah took a sharp breath, as if she'd been hit in the stomach. Hattie felt that way herself as she stared at them both. Indian? They were Indian?

Enah shook her head, and her mouth trembled.

"The folks that camped near us were Caddo Indians," Gramma said gently. "My parents had just homesteaded our place in Texas, and the Caddo moved there after selling their land in Louisiana."

"Selling?" Enah's eyes flashed. "They were *forced* to leave. There was money given and a paper signed, but they had no choice."

"I know," said Gramma. "It was hard for them to move and start over. My folks made friends with them and did some trading with them since they were the closest neighbors we had. Mama would take me to the camp with her, and I played stickball with the children. Mama learned a lot from the women about plants for healing. She'd go home and write things down. When I got older, she taught me."

Gramma fingered the scraper. "The women wore hairpieces like your granddaughter gave Hattie. When she first brought it home, I couldn't remember, but now it's all clear. They carved spoons from deer horns, used glass scrapers, and could fix corn

127

more ways than I could count. I should've figured out sooner who you were."

Enah shook her head. "It's better if no one knows."

Hattie had to speak or burst wide open. "Not even your kids?"

"No!" said Enah. "The old ways are gone. For my people, the Caddo Adais, the old ways were gone long before the other Caddo left for Texas. Do you know why?" she demanded.

Gramma and Hattie shook their heads.

"Long ago, before white men came, my people lived here. We farmed and traveled the rivers and traded with others; the men hunted. We were friends to the Spanish and the French. The mission at Los Adais was built by the priests who taught us to know Jesus and to live as Christians.

"My grandfather said that for a time our life was not a bad thing. Then more whites came with their wars and diseases. The Spanish fought the French, and then the Americans, for land that didn't belong to any of them."

Enah was breathing hard and had to stop. For long moments Hattie could hear only Enah's labored breaths and the bubbling of the corn.

"I'm surprised you were able to stay here," Gramma said.

"The Spanish made land grants to our people," Enah said. "But we had to take new names. 'Varga' is a Spanish name, after a man my grandfather knew. As times got worse, most Indians were killed or taken away or made to work as slaves. The wise ones of the Adais said that if we were to keep our land, we must live quietly in the white man's way. So the old ways were buried. In many families the children were told they were Spanish. In others, the truth is known but never spoken of."

"What did your parents tell you?" Hattie asked.

"I knew we were Caddo," Enah said. "But when I was a little girl and the land north of us was sold in the treaty, they were afraid the Americans would want ours next. My mother made me promise never to speak the old words or tell who we were." Enah sank back, and huge tears wandered like streams down the creases of her face. "Sometimes I've broken that promise and used the old words. The children don't know what they mean, but it comforts me to hear them."

"So no one bothered you all this time?" asked Gramma.

"People gave us looks when we went to town," Enah said bitterly. "But no one came here. We would hear terrible news about our brothers in Texas, and we were thankful we had stayed."

Gramma nodded. "It was bad in some places. More settlers poured in when Texas became a state, and the Apache and Comanche were fighting back real hard. Indians got blamed for every missing hog and human being, no matter what tribe they were from. Most Texans wanted to get rid of them all."

Gramma shook her head sadly. "That's when our

Caddo neighbors had to leave. For a while, when it was too dangerous for them to trade elsewhere, my father would buy extra supplies in town and trade with them. Then the camp was discovered, and in just one night they were gone. Mama and I didn't even get to say goodbye."

"What happened to them?" asked Hattie.

"The Indian agent, Robert Neighbors, took them west to a reservation out on the Brazos River. But things got worse, so in '59 he moved them to Indian territory in Oklahoma. I remember seeing it in the newspaper. The Caddo were finally safe, but Mr. Neighbors was shot in the back by a white man."

Hattie pondered all that she was hearing. She had always been so proud of her pioneer heritage, but it hurt hearing this side of the story. How could she be proud of this?

"Are you ever going to tell your kids?" she asked Enah.

"They have to live in a white man's world," said Enah. "It's better this way."

"The wars are over," said Gramma. "It's not the same now."

Enah shook her head. "When Regina went to school, she was teased and made to sit in the back of the room. They didn't even know she was Indian— she was just different."

"She really misses being with young people," said Hattie.

Enah nodded sadly. "I know. It's time for her to

go to Spanish Lake and find a husband. Some of our people live there and farm as we do. She will fit in."

A sob choked the woman. "I must do this while there is still time, but my heart breaks to see her go."

Suddenly Hattie felt like crying, too, as sorrow for Regina flooded out the jealousy she had felt before. She reached out to grasp Enah's hand.

"Ma'am, I know you don't think much of me, but Regina's my friend, and I don't think you're being fair. She has a right to know who she is and to marry who . . ." Hattie almost choked on this part. ". . . to marry whomever she wants."

The old woman tensed as she stared at Hattie. Then her face softened.

"You're wrong, little one. I think a great deal of you. At first I was afraid that you would bring us trouble. But your heart is kind, and you're a good friend to my children." She gripped Hattie's hand. "Now, I will trust you not to tell them what you know. If they learn this, it should be from me."

"That means you'll tell them?"

"It means I will pray for wisdom," Enah said with a long, weary sigh.

"Why don't you run outside now?" Gramma suggested to Hattie.

Hattie stood to go. "Mrs. Enah, I'll be praying, too," she said.

The women looked at each other, and Gramma smiled.

"What's funny?" asked Hattie.

"Nothing," explained Gramma. "It's just that 'enah' isn't a name like 'Hattie.' It's the Caddo word for 'mother.'"

Hattie thought a minute about how strange it must sound to be called Mrs. Mother. "What is your real name?" she asked Enah.

"My Christian name is Lucia," Enah said softly. "But when I was small, my grandfather called me Iwi, 'the eagle.' His eyes were growing poor, but mine were very sharp."

"Iwi," said Hattie. "That's a wonderful name. If you were my grandmother, I'd want to know that." Then she scooted out the door.

14

Confessions

After Gramma had stirred up a pot of her "medicinal" chicken soup, and the others finished repairing the garden, it was time to go. Uncle Burl was much impressed with his neighbors' assortment of crops and was puzzled that he hadn't met the Vargas before. In return for the help, Lou sent them home with a side of venison and a gourd vine.

"Until that heifer of yours starts giving milk for the young'uns, I'll be glad to swap for some more of those squash," Uncle Burl told Lou. "Just send the boy over."

Lou agreed. Goodbyes were brief since Gramma promised to check on her patient the next day. Though Hattie hadn't talked to Eric since they arrived, she had a sudden urge to tell him Enah's story.

As they bounced onto the main road, she whispered to Gramma, "I promised Enah not to tell the kids her secret, but she didn't say anything about Eric. Do you think it's okay?"

Glancing up at Uncle Burl, Gramma shook her head. "Not now."

It was a long ride back to the farm. There was so much more that Hattie wanted to ask Gramma about the Caddo, but all she could do was think and wonder. And then there was the matter of Eric and Regina. Hattie sighed. It was hard knowing what to feel anymore.

The sun was gone, and the western sky was tinged with orange when they reached the house. After tending Aunt Millie and all six kids for the afternoon, Mama was frazzled. So, despite her own weariness, Gramma finished cooking supper while Hattie, Eric, and Uncle Burl did chores until bedtime. There was no time to talk.

The next day was the same. After Eric spent the morning hoeing cotton, Uncle Burl agreed to let him drive Gramma over to check Enah. Hattie was following them out the door when Mama called her.

"Whoa, girl. I really need you today. Gramma can do her doctoring just fine alone."

"But, Mama . . ." Hattie pleaded.

"I mean it, Hattie," said Mama. "I want to finish canning Millie's tomatoes before we go home. Maybe next time."

Hattie had a long face as she watched the wagon leave. So they were going home soon. Not long ago she would have been thrilled. Now she couldn't bear the thought of saying goodbye. But maybe it was just as well. How could she talk to Regina now without telling what she knew?

The wagon rumbled back in just before dark. Hattie met Gramma on the porch. "How's Enah doing?" she asked.

"She's a little stronger today," said Gramma, sinking into a rocker.

"Has she told them?" Hattie whispered.

Gramma shook her head.

"I don't understand," said Hattie. "It's not fair having to grow up not knowing who you are."

"Then try to understand that Enah has lived with fear all her life," Gramma explained. "She's trying to protect her family from people who have treated Indians cruelly."

"I know," said Hattie. "That bothers me, too, Gramma. I've always been so proud of who we are, but it sounds like we just came in and stole all this land. How could Christian people do that?"

Gramma sighed. "That's a hard question, honey. My papa used to ask the same thing."

She thought a while, then went on slowly, as if searching for the right words. "First of all, some people who call themselves Christian don't even know what that means. But you can be sure of one thing," Gramma said, wagging her finger, "those who hurt other folks while wearing Christ's name will have to answer to Him—mark my word, they will."

She leaned back in the chair. "You must also remember that folks came here for all kinds of reasons. There were missionaries who were willing to give their lives to tell people about Jesus, while others just saw a chance to get rich. And a few just wanted adventure. Then others, like my folks, were having a hard time and wanted a new life. My papa was a good man who never meant to hurt anyone or take what wasn't his. In such a big land it seemed there should've been room for everyone."

"That's what I think," said Hattie. "Back home you can ride for miles and not see a soul."

"If we all loved each other and lived by the Golden Rule like my papa did, there would have been room," said Gramma. "But as it turned out, the land wasn't big enough for the different ways of life, or for folks who couldn't understand each other. And there's never enough room for greedy men, Hattie. As long as there's been people, someone's always wanted more than he had."

"I guess I can't blame Enah for the way she used to look at me," said Hattie.

"It's hard for her to trust white people," agreed Gramma.

"If she tells the kids about being Caddo, do you think Regina will still want to be my friend?"

"She may see herself in a new light, but I doubt it will change how she feels about you," said Gramma.

"I doubt it'll change how she feels about Eric either," Hattie mumbled.

"Does that bother you?" asked Gramma.

"It shouldn't. I keep saying that Eric and I are just friends and that it wouldn't matter if he had a girlfriend." Hattie sighed. "But it does matter."

"Why is that?" Gramma inquired.

"Well, first Sam and I were real close until he met Lorene and decided to ride off on that dumb cattle drive before they get married. Then Eric came along, and we've had such a good time this summer. He was getting to be a really good friend—until we came here."

"Now you're having to share him, too."

Hattie nodded. "Gramma, I don't mean to be selfish, but it hurts to lose friends."

"We all want to be special to someone, Hattie, when they're special to us. But we have to be careful about jealousy. The Bible says that jealousy rots the bones." Gramma reached out to squeeze her granddaughter's hand. "Keep praying for your friends. It's nearly impossible to pray for someone and think unkindly about them at the same time."

Four days, six washpots of clothes, and thirty-two quarts of tomatoes later, Mama said it was time to leave. Aunt Millie's lungs were clear, and she was growing stronger each day. Clovis and Pearl were well enough to resume their chores. And thanks to Eric's help, Uncle Burl had the crops in good shape again.

When Gramma was ready to check on Enah one

last time, Hattie was allowed to go along. She sat in the back of the wagon with Gramma while Eric drove.

"Why don't you sit up there with the driver?" suggested Gramma.

Hattie shook her head.

Using her cane, Gramma gave Hattie's shin a friendly nudge.

Reluctantly, Hattie climbed onto the wagon seat beside Eric. They rode in silence until she could stand it no longer.

"I guess you're glad to be going home," she said.

"I guess."

"I'm going to miss it here though," Hattie went on. "Aunt Millie's kids kind of grow on you, and it'll be hard saying goodbye to the Vargas."

"You'll be back sometime," said Eric.

"What about you?"

He looked at her. "That depends on if I'm invited."

"Oh," said Hattie. "I thought maybe you planned to keep in touch with Regina."

Eric sighed. "I was wondering when you'd get around to her."

Hattie's face got hot. How dare he read her mind? She glanced back at Gramma, who was humming softly as she dug in her medicine bag, pretending not to hear them. Oh well, Gramma knew everything anyway. Hattie took a deep breath and plunged on.

"Eric, I've been a little touchy where Regina's concerned, but that was selfish and I'm sorry. You can even kiss her goodbye if you want, and I won't say a word—I won't even look. Whoever you have for a girlfriend or marry someday is up to you. I just hope that we can always be friends. You're very . . . you're very special to me."

For a second Hattie thought he was going to drop the reins. Then he gripped them tightly and turned to stare at her.

"Hattie Marshall, you beat everything."

She stared back, wondering what *that* meant.

"Regina's a nice girl, and she's going through a tough time, but she's no closer to me than to you," said Eric. "Why do you think I came here in the first place?"

Hattie shrugged. "To study chicken pox and get away from home for a while, I suppose."

"Wrong," said Eric. Glancing back at Gramma, his face turned a little red, and his dark eyebrows knit together in a frown. Then he took a deep breath and dropped his voice so low that Hattie could barely hear him. "I came to be with you."

Hattie couldn't speak or even look at him. She couldn't stop thinking about their arguments and her fretting about Regina. Then a happy, relieved little tear crept down her cheek. Quickly she wiped it away, but not before Eric had noticed and reached over to hold her hand.

Behind them, Gramma kept humming.

It was quiet at the Varga place. This concerned Hattie until Inez ran to greet them from the chicken house, one egg bouncing out of her basket as she scurried toward them.

"Inez! Be careful with those eggs!" Regina shouted from the door. Then she waved. "Hattie, it's good to see you. We've been hoping you could come back."

"Mama's kept me busy," said Hattie as she hopped out of the wagon. "But I had to come one more time. We're going home tomorrow."

"Oh." Regina's face fell. "I had hoped we could go back to the creek once Enah gets better."

"I expect we'll be back next year," said Hattie. "Mama and Aunt Millie can't get along without seeing each other every few months."

"I may not be here then," said Regina.

"Why?" asked Hattie and Eric together.

"It's a long story," she said. "First come in to see Enah. She's been asking about you."

They followed Regina inside, where Gramma was already tasting a pot of red deer meat chili. The delicious smell filled the cabin and made Hattie's stomach growl.

Enah sat propped on her bed, her pewter-colored hair neatly combed to fall like a mantle across her shoulders. The golden color of her skin was almost back to normal, and her eyes were bright. She motioned for Hattie to sit by the bed.

"How are you feeling?" Hattie asked.

"Like maybe I'm not ready for *Kee-wut-hi-u*," said Enah.

Hattie stared at her.

Enah smiled. "That means heaven. I'm not going yet. There is too much to do here. Did Regina tell you?"

"No, ma'am."

"When I'm stronger, we're going to visit our people at Spanish Lake. Some are Regina's age, and she should get to know them," Enah said with a wink.

Hattie looked at Regina, wondering how she felt about this.

"Enah has told us some things about our people that we didn't know," Regina said. There was a new glow in her dark eyes. "I'm glad we're going."

"That's right," added Inez, bouncing as usual. "She says we are Caddo Adais, a very special people who know how to keep secrets. Now that we're big enough, Enah's going to teach us about being Indian. She knows all kinds of stories and songs. And she told us she's been playing tricks on us with the old words. Did you know that *deetsi* means 'dog' and *oot* means 'raccoon'?"

"And that *enah* means 'mother'?" Regina added.

Hattie smiled at Inez and Regina, then at Enah. "I'm so glad you told them!"

Enah nodded and clasped her hands to her chest.

"A great weight is gone from my heart. If God is willing, perhaps I will last a little longer. There is so much to tell my children."

Hattie reached out to hug her. "I honor you, Mother Iwi," she whispered. "You have done a brave thing."

Enah smiled at the sound of her old name and kissed Hattie's cheek. "As my children will listen and learn from me, so you must listen to your grandmother. She has many things to teach you."

"Yes, ma'am," agreed Hattie, wiping the tears from her eyes. Turning to go, she noticed Eric. The mystified look on his face made her smile.

"Come on, *amigo*," she said, taking his arm, then Regina's. "It's a *long* story."

Author's Note

This story is fictional. The Caddo Adais, however, are very real. Their ancestors were among the first to greet Spanish explorers in Louisiana and Texas. Caught between Spanish and French colonists, the Adais coped with both without shedding white blood.

As Louisiana and Texas became states, most Native American groups were moved around or taken to Indian territory in Oklahoma—but not the Adais. Living quietly on Spanish land grants, they adopted European names, speech, and dress. Because they did this so well, they were not forced out with other Caddo groups.

But there was a price. Like many native groups who adopted the white man's ways, later generations of Adais knew little about their culture. Some families, fearing more trouble, had kept their identity a secret. Others lost it completely.

In the 1970s, descendants of the Adais began to research their heritage. Many still lived in Louisiana and East Texas. They became recognized by the state of Louisiana in 1993. With the help of Caddo relatives in Oklahoma, the Adais are learning about their culture again and are teaching it to their children. The Adais whom I have come to know have been warm and generous with their help. I wish them well.

I offer special thanks to Chief Rufus Davis, Pat Wray Applewhite, and Dr. Claude McCrocklin, the archaeologist who graciously shared his findings at a Caddo homesite. Appreciation also goes to Donna Medlin, Debbie Johnston, and Teri Copponex, my partners of the trail.